USBORNE READER'S LIBRARY

TALES OF REAL HEROISM

Paul Dowsv

Designed by
Nigel Reece, Karen Tomlins
and Helen Westwood

Illustrated by Ian Jackson
and
Aziz Khan, Janos Marffy, Guy Smith,
Ross Watton and Sean Wilkinson

Contents

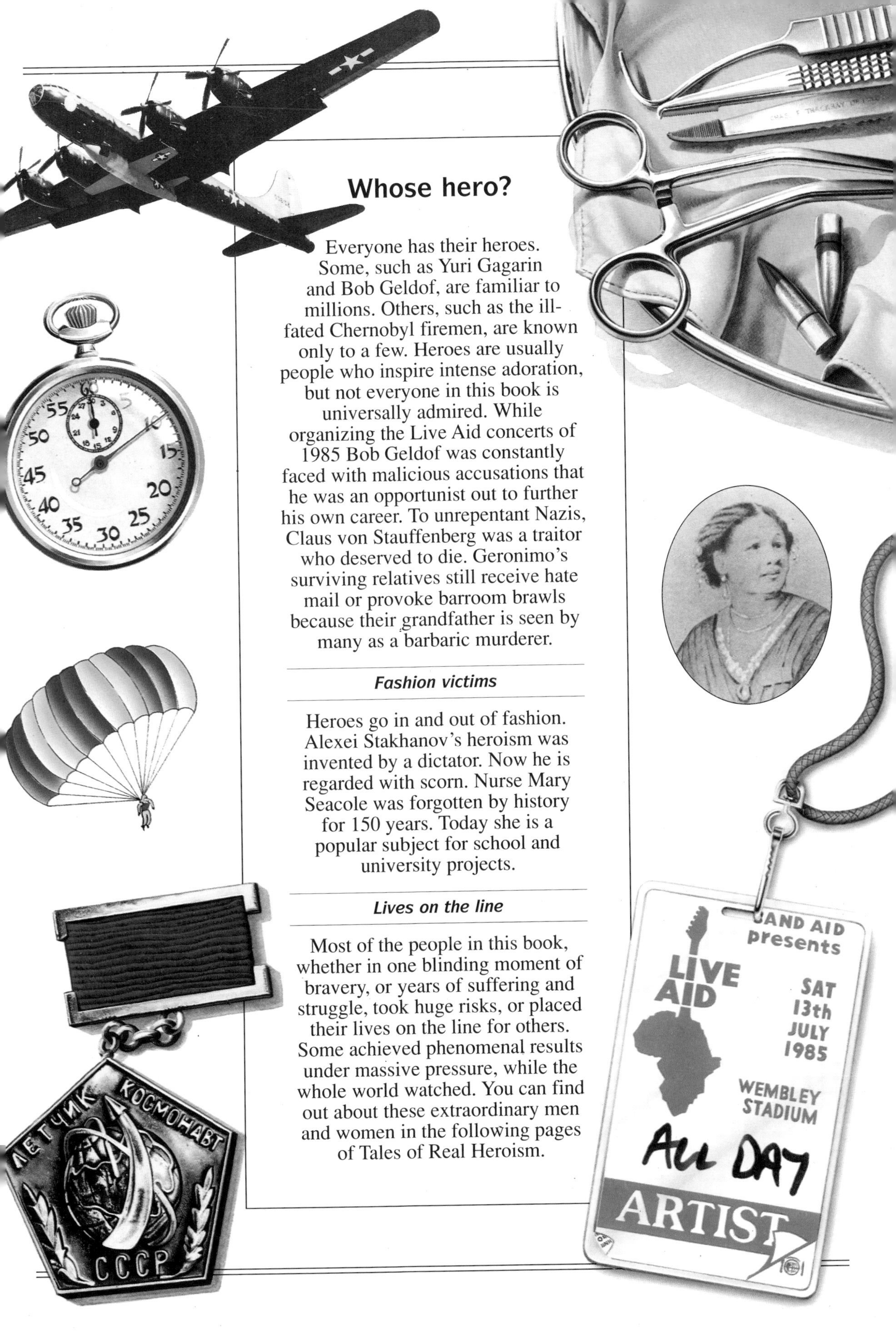

Whose hero?

Everyone has their heroes. Some, such as Yuri Gagarin and Bob Geldof, are familiar to millions. Others, such as the ill-fated Chernobyl firemen, are known only to a few. Heroes are usually people who inspire intense adoration, but not everyone in this book is universally admired. While organizing the Live Aid concerts of 1985 Bob Geldof was constantly faced with malicious accusations that he was an opportunist out to further his own career. To unrepentant Nazis, Claus von Stauffenberg was a traitor who deserved to die. Geronimo's surviving relatives still receive hate mail or provoke barroom brawls because their grandfather is seen by many as a barbaric murderer.

Fashion victims

Heroes go in and out of fashion. Alexei Stakhanov's heroism was invented by a dictator. Now he is regarded with scorn. Nurse Mary Seacole was forgotten by history for 150 years. Today she is a popular subject for school and university projects.

Lives on the line

Most of the people in this book, whether in one blinding moment of bravery, or years of suffering and struggle, took huge risks, or placed their lives on the line for others. Some achieved phenomenal results under massive pressure, while the whole world watched. You can find out about these extraordinary men and women in the following pages of Tales of Real Heroism.

Boomtown Bob's global jukebox

In October, 1984, BBC News reporter Michael Buerk and a small camera crew wandered around a dusty plain in Ethiopia. Packed around them, as far as the eye could see, were an unfathomable number of emaciated refugees. They had gathered here to be fed by a European charity.

Reporting for the evening news, Buerk patiently described the combination of civil war and drought that had led so many starving people to congregate in this hellish place. The camera closed in on a young aid-worker whose job it was to select from the waiting thousands a few hundred to be fed. Those chosen were ushered into a small compound and given a simple meal.

Ethiopia was already extremely poor before the civil war and famine of the 1980s.

It was barely enough, even for them, but it would keep them alive for another day. Those who had not been selected waited outside the compound, condemned to watch others eat, while they starved to death.

Boomtown Bob

Watching this report at his London home was pop star Bob Geldof, singer with Dublin's Boomtown Rats. The group had had great success in the late 1970s and early 1980s, but now no one was buying their records. Geldof had spent a dispiriting day trying to promote their latest single to a disinterested media, but what he was seeing on TV made his own problems seem insignificant. To Geldof, the people he watched looked like beings from another planet. Their limbs were skeleton-thin, and from their shrunken heads huge vacant eyes stared out at him.

That night Geldof lay awake haunted by the images he had seen, and felt a mounting

Bob Geldof in 1985. The Dublin singer had made many friends in the music business, and was well placed to organize the Band Aid and Live Aid projects.

Refugees were fed a mixture of oats, powdered milk and sugar.

As famine swept through Ethiopia and Sudan thousands of refugees gathered at feeding stations such as this.

indignation that such a catastrophe had been allowed to happen.

He wondered what he could do. Perhaps he could record a song with other pop musicians, and give the profits to Ethiopia. A sociable and charismatic character, Geldof had made many friends in the music business, so the next day he began phoning as many as he dared.

Eager to help

Many of those contacted had seen Michael Buerk's report and were eager to help. In one afternoon Geldof had roped in an impressive handful of famous British pop musicians. Now all he needed was a song.

He had the germ of a tune, and the words came to him in the back of a taxi. He scribbled them down in his diary, and when he played the song to a positive reception, Geldof knew he had something that would work.

Everything for free

The idea picked up an unstoppable momentum. His record company pledged their support, and before the song was even completed he had persuaded everybody involved to donate their services for free.

Usually, the retailer made the greatest profit. In the United Kingdom almost all records were sold in one of six chain stores. Geldof rang each in turn, telling them they were the last on his list and that their five competitors had agreed not to take a share of the profits. Naturally, all agreed, not wanting to be singled out as the one company who had put profit before charity.

Spending day after day seemingly glued to a telephone, Geldof persuaded ICI, the huge British chemical company, to contribute the vinyl material to make the record, and ZTT studio to donate free recording time. Eventually the entire cost of the record was covered by companies and individuals giving their time and material for free.

Sunday November 25 was chosen as the recording day, and aided by his friend and fellow musician Midge Ure, Geldof rushed to complete his song. It was called *Do they know it's Christmas?* and the musicians recording it would be called Band Aid.

Record costs

In 1984 most pop music was sold on vinyl discs. A single record cost £1.30. The money would be shared out as shown below.

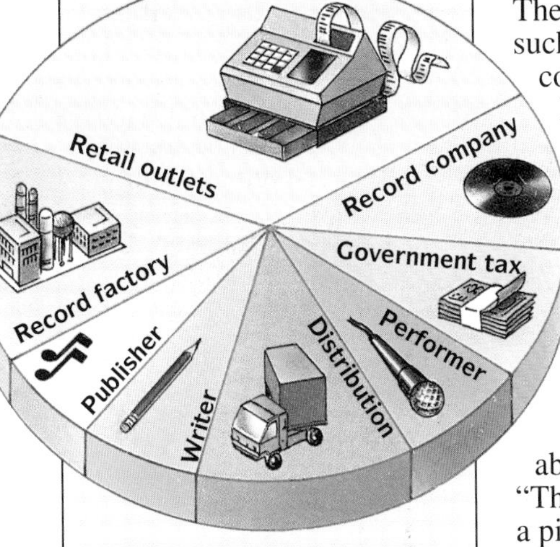

Geldof persuaded all those involved in the project to donate both time and material for free. At first the British government was unwilling to waive their tax, but eventually relented.

Band Aid day

At the recording the most famous stars took turns to sing a couple of lines from each verse, while the rest played or sang along in the catchy football-crowd-like chorus. The publicity that surrounded such a gathering, and the concern in the country for the Ethiopian famine, made success inevitable, but its scale was surprising.

Unflagging crusade

Geldof pushed the song unflaggingly on TV and radio, and his crusade to make as much money as possible took on an abrasive edge. "The price of a life this year is a piece of plastic with a hole in the middle," he told radio listeners. "How many more children will you let die in your living room before you act... Even if you hate the song, buy it and throw it away."

It became the United Kingdom's biggest selling

Geldof persuaded renowned British artist Peter Blake to create a cover for *Do they know it's Christmas?*. Blake's most famous work was the cover of The Beatles' *Sergeant Pepper* album.

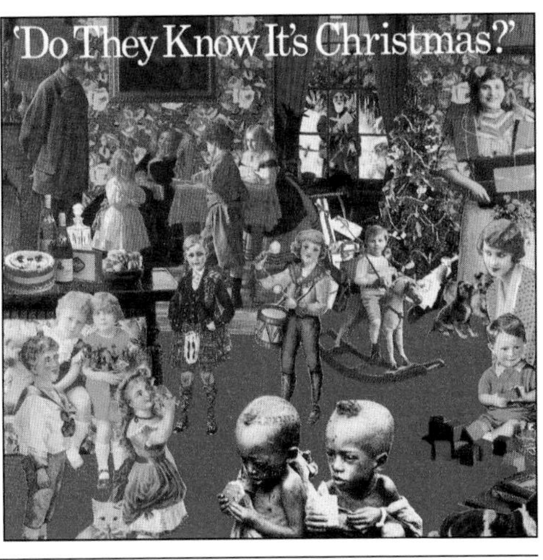

single ever. Over 3.6 million copies were sold in the UK (8.1 million were sold internationally). Some people even bought the record by the box, and sent them as Christmas cards.

Direct aid

By January, the record had raised over £5 million. Wondering how best to spend it, Geldof spoke to several well-known charities, but all said they would have to take a substantial part of the money to cover administration costs. But Geldof had promised the public that every penny they spent on his record would go directly to feed starving people. He also began to feel that, as the money had come from all over the world, then no single country should have access to it. It became apparent that the best thing to do would be to go to Ethiopia himself, to see how best to spend it.

He could not afford to pay for the trip, so he persuaded a TV station and tabloid newspaper to pay for a flight to the Ethiopian capital Addis Ababa, and a hotel. The press followed him out. Millions had contributed to Band Aid, and the newspapers knew these people were desperate to know what Geldof was doing with their money.

Blunt talk

Once in Addis Ababa Geldof was characteristically blunt about what he thought needed to be done. He was beginning to realize Band Aid had a unique opportunity to do something special. Unlike a government, he was offering aid without expecting anything in return. Unlike a charity, he did not have to worry about keeping up long-term good relations with local politicians.

The next day Geldof and a horde of British newspaper men were taken to a feeding station at Lalibela to witness the famine first hand. Geldof was determined not to give the newspapers the photograph they all wanted – "Saint Bob" (as the press had jokingly begun to call him) comforting a starving child. Not everyone respected his wishes, but most photographers were too shocked to take pictures, sensing these children deserved more than to be the subject of a sentimental photograph. The trip was useful. Geldof was able to speak face to face with aid workers and make direct contact with the people he intended to help.

From Ethiopia he also visited Sudan, where a crisis as serious as that in Ethiopia was now brewing.

Geldof with Ethiopian families during his trip in January, 1985.

World concert

Geldof returned to Britain with a burning anger, and the solid awareness that Band Aid needed an appropriate organization to administer the money it had made. He recruited a collection of well-respected government and media figures as a board of directors, and an office was set up, where, in the spirit of Band Aid, all equipment was donated.

Bad news soon poured into the office. In early 1985 there were 22 million people starving to death. The £8 million raised so far would be enough to keep them alive for two weeks. But Geldof had another more audacious idea to bring money to both Ethiopia and Sudan. The Band Aid concept had been taken up all over the world, with many countries recording their own famine relief song. A global concert could be the next step.

Geldof envisaged a concert in Britain, at the same time as a concert in the United States, broadcast around the world, with acts alternating on either stage. Between sets there would be constant appeals for money, and people could phone in with credit card donations, or promises to send money via their bank accounts. It would be the biggest concert in history, and hopefully it would raise a massive amount of money. The idea was to become known as Live Aid.

The Boomtown Rats were touring in early 1985. The day after the tour ended Geldof rang Wembley stadium in London, and booked it for Saturday July 13. He had 20 weeks to organize the event.

As with the record, Geldof had no problem recruiting acts to perform. The most renowned names in pop volunteered their services, and famous groups which had split up offered to get back together for the day. Before the week was out Geldof was contemplating an event featuring about fifty acts, each one performing their most popular songs for 15-20 minutes. It would be like a "global jukebox" he explained. In that way no one watching would get bored and switch off. The more who watched, the more who could be persuaded to donate money.

Goldsmith and Graham

Although the idea was fraught with potential catastrophe Geldof had two huge aces up his sleeve. Britain's foremost pop promoter Harvey Goldsmith had offered his services. He was well respected and a brilliant organizer. In the United States, Bill Graham, an equally prestigious pop promoter, was also recruited. With fourteen weeks to go, the involvement of both men reassured would-be performers that the event was unlikely to be a shambles.

But problems were mounting. The owners of Wembley stadium were demanding £150,000 for its use. Geldof wanted the venue for free. American singer Bruce Springsteen was playing there the day before. Although he was uncertain about whether to perform, he had already agreed to let Live Aid use his stage and amplification equipment. This, despite the cost, was one good reason to use Wembley. The owners were bartered down to £100,000, and the venue was confirmed.

TV headache

Persuading TV stations to broadcast the concert was not as easy as Geldof hoped. As well as making money from the viewers he also intended to charge the TV stations for taking the concert. However, it would last about 17 hours, and most companies thought this was too long. Rearranging their schedules would also cost any TV company a substantial amount in cancellation fees. Eight weeks before the concert there was still no TV coverage lined up. Without it the concerts would be a waste of time.

But in late May, the BBC agreed to broadcast. Shortly afterwards Ireland agreed to broadcast Live Aid in its entirety, and the European TV companies came on board. But in the USA, there was still no agreement.

Further problems were coming from Wembley. The catering company there was refusing to donate their profits. With everyone else working for free to help starving people, it seemed obscene that a food company should be the only one making a profit. Geldof threatened to ask everyone to bring their own food. "I don't think you can do that" said the company. "I can do what I like, pal" Geldof bristled, and sure enough, that was what he did.

But there were triumphs too. The London police agreed to attend the event for free, saving the organizers many thousands of pounds. Throughout the UK, companies with large switchboards volunteered to operate them during the concert, so people could phone in pledges.

With only a few weeks before the concert, there was still no US venue, so Geldof flew to the States to straighten

The Band Aid Logo (background) of a round map of the world like a plate with a knife and fork, was Geldof's idea.

Transporting food from the UK to Africa was vastly expensive. So instead of paying the cost of hiring ships to transport goods to Ethiopia, Band Aid leased several boats long-term to take both their goods, and the supplies of other charities.

things out. The city of Philadelphia offered its John F. Kennedy stadium. The Live Aid organizers would have preferred a more well-known and easily accessible venue, but at least this one was free.

The press conference to announce the event was held the day after Philadelphia was confirmed as the location for the US concert. Geldof was now exhausted. Weeks of cajoling and blustering his way through phone calls and meetings, and the round of nonstop journeys had drained him. But whenever his will to go on wavered, the images he had seen on TV would return to haunt him.

Almost every famous pop star from the previous 25 years was on the Live Aid bill. Geldof was also able to tell the press what his organization had been doing. Two Band Aid ships loaded with food and medicine were sailing for Ethiopia. Food was already being flown there. Band Aid was also negotiating to buy a fleet of their own trucks as African trucking companies usually charged extortionate prices to transport food to trouble spots.

Cash from chaos

Tickets for Wembley sold out in three days, but problems still loomed with television coverage. Many European stations seemed to be treating the event as a pop concert, rather than a money-raising exercise. Geldof threatened to withdraw their right to broadcast unless they organized appropriate money-collecting facilities.

In the United States, things were still chaotic. With three weeks to go, Geldof and Harvey Goldsmith flew out to see what was going on.

Although the venue had been decided, there were no tickets on sale. There was no final bill of artists. Even the stage plans (vital to ensure a quick turn around of the large number of acts) had been lost.

They also discovered that, apart from the performers, almost everyone else expected to be paid. The stage sound, lighting, and television technicians, stadium security staff and others would cost $3.5 million. (Wembley, by comparison, would only cost $250,000.) However, the Pepsi-Cola company, and others, had agreed to sponsor the Philadelphia show, and their money covered the stadium's huge costs.

Pulled apart

As the date grew nearer, the pressure on Geldof increased. Sponsors and television companies wrangled for special privileges or made unreasonable demands in return for their services. The American network ABC for example demanded that all the biggest stars should perform during one three-hour slot, when they estimated that most people would be watching.

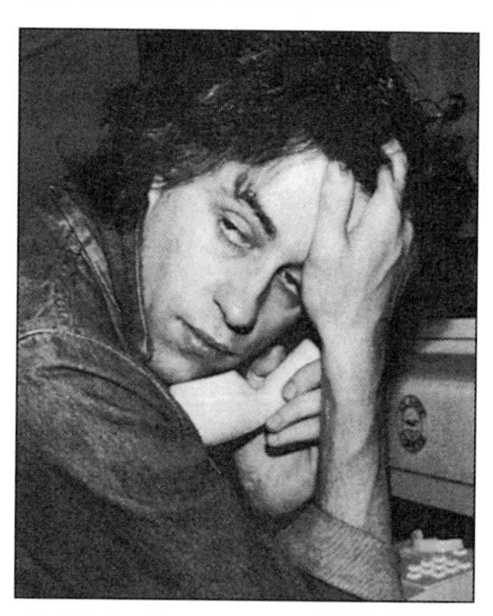

Geldof, glued to a telephone, in the final run up to the concert.

Geldof felt that he was being pulled apart. Massively overworked, he could not even sleep, as phone calls from Australia and California (where there is a nine to ten hour time difference) came in throughout the night.

He was plagued by a fear of failure. At night he lay awake bathed in cold sweat. If he did sleep, he would wake at six, his stomach in a knot. There were no contracts with the performers. If pop stars began to suspect things were going wrong, they would pull out. The concert would collapse, and Geldof would look like the world's biggest charlatan.

Moving mountains

But there were promising signals. Performers were moving mountains to be there. The Prince and Princess of Wales had agreed to attend. The BBC had found 500 telephone lines around the UK that could be used to take donations.

The night before the concert Geldof went to bed early with an aching back. At 2:00am the phone rang. It was an American manager threatening to pull out unless his group was given more time to perform. "******* pull out then," snapped Geldof, "I'm going to bed."

Live Aid day

Backpain kept him awake half the night, but Geldof woke the next day to a beautiful sunny morning. Driving through the streets of London en route to Wembley, passers-by shouted their good wishes, and he could sense that history was being made. If all went according to plan 85 percent of the world's television sets would be tuned into the concert.

At Wembley, he was relieved to see that the acts who had agreed to perform were actually turning up. Until then, the only group Geldof knew for certain would play was his own, and, as he put it, "17 hours of the Boomtown Rats would be too much for anybody."

Blur

The day passed in a blur – the Prince and Princess of Wales, the band of Guardsmen starting the concert with the national anthem, his own performance where he told the 80,000 Wembley crowd "This is the best day of my life", his TV interview afterward where he swore at British viewers for not sending enough money (donations soared shortly afterward), the Arab oil sheikh who donated £1 million.

Finale

Such was the improvised nature of the day that although the schedule proclaimed "Finale" at the end of the concert, nothing had actually been rehearsed. Geldof, now in considerable pain with a trapped nerve in his back, gathered as many performers as he could to rehearse *"Do they know it's Christmas?"* at the back of the stage.

As they ran through the song with an unamplified electric guitar the power failed and they carried on in the dark.

At 10:00pm the concert finished with a ragged but glorious version of the song. Geldof, who had fallen asleep from sheer exhaustion moments before, was hoisted onto the shoulders of rock's greatest performers, and the Wembley crowd shouted out the chorus of "Feed the World" to a global audience of one and a half billion people.

Rocking all over the world

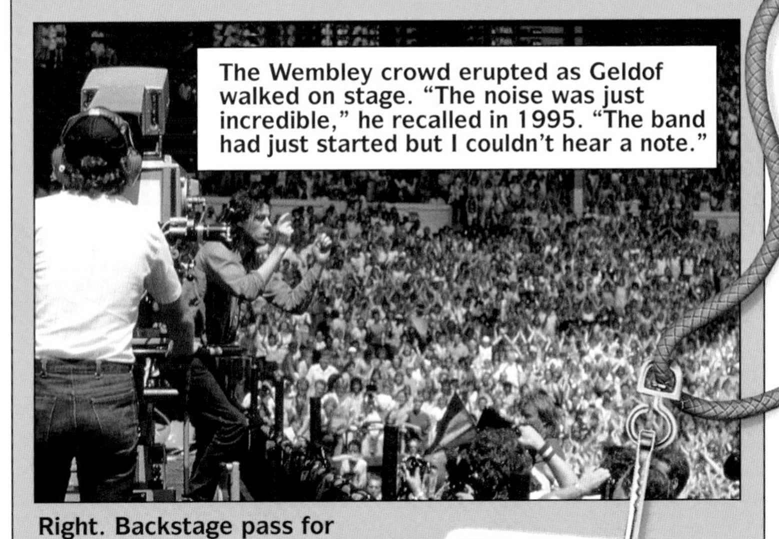

The Wembley crowd erupted as Geldof walked on stage. "The noise was just incredible," he recalled in 1995. "The band had just started but I couldn't hear a note."

Right. Backstage pass for Wembley stadium.

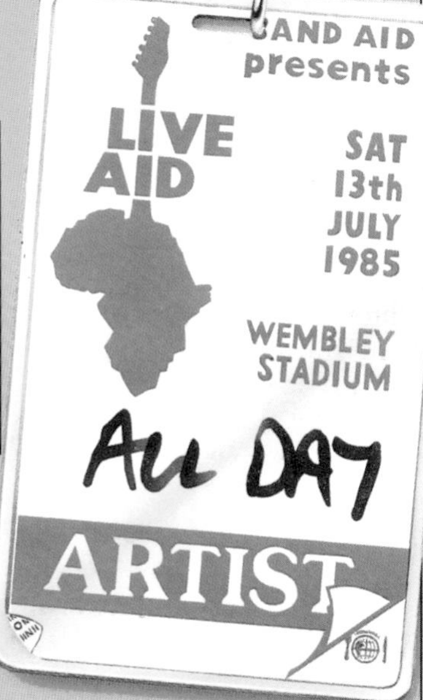

Below. Eric Clapton performs for the Philadelphia crowd.

Below. Live Aid performers sing *"Do they know it's Christmas?"* as the British leg of the concert draws to an end. Pictured with Geldof, alongside other performers, are George Michael, former Beatle Paul McCartney, Elton John and Sting.

Punching a hole in the sky

In the summer of 1947 a huge silver B-29 bomber soared off the windswept runway at Muroc Airbase, California. As it climbed into a cloudless August sky, the sun gleamed brightly on a strange bullet-shaped aircraft slung under its belly. This was the Bell X-1 rocket, a machine designed to fly beyond the known frontiers of aviation science.

The X-1's pilot, a 24-year-old US Air Force captain named Chuck Yeager, knew he was gambling with death every time he took to the sky. But before the year was out, Yeager was determined to fly this rocket beyond the speed of sound – faster than any man had ever flown before.

In 1947 supersonic* flight was dark, forbidding territory. Yeager joked that it might make his ears fall off, but some aircraft attempting to break the sound barrier had literally disintegrated – shaken apart by invisible forces no one understood. Most aviation engineers believed no aircraft could fly faster than sound. They believed there was a "sound barrier" – an invisible wall of turbulence that would tear apart any plane that tried to break through it.

Flying helmet. Yeager wore a steel hard hat over his helmet to protect his head during the turbulent X-1 flights.

Dangerous missions such as these were rarely flown by military pilots. A highly paid civilian test pilot named "Slick" Goodlin had begun the project. As the X-1 tests approached the speed of sound, he demanded a $150,000 bonus for an actual attempt on the sound barrier. The United States military could no longer afford him, and decided to recruit a pilot from within their own ranks.

Despite the obvious dangers, Yeager volunteered. Flying filled him with an indescribable joy. The chance to pilot a beautiful aircraft like the X-1 was heaven sent. Besides, in the competitive world of the test pilot, the opportunity to become the first man to travel faster than sound was too good to miss. He took the job on his standard captain's pay of $283 a month.

Oddball

With his slow West Virginian country drawl, Yeager was something of an oddball in the high-powered world of experimental flying, but his exceptional skill and quick thinking coolness under pressure made him the best test pilot at Muroc.

Now, on this breezy August

Speed of sound

Supersonic speed is measured in Mach numbers, after the Austrian physicist Ernst Mach who first measured it. The speed of sound is known as Mach 1. Mach .5 is half the speed of sound.

*Faster than sound.

day Yeager was about to pilot the X-1 on his first powered flight. He had flown the plane before, but only on glide flights. This time it was brimming with liquid oxygen and alcohol fuel.

At the flick of a rocket ignition switch his craft could shoot straight to the top of the sky, or it could explode into a thousand flaming pieces. He was nervous, but told himself fear was the pilot's friend. It sharpened the senses and kept the mind focused on the job he had to do.

Small stages

Attempting to break through the sound barrier was so dangerous it would only be attempted in small stages. The X-1 would be dropped from the bomb bay at 8,000m (25,000ft) and then Yeager would ignite the rockets, and fly off into the horizon. Being unleashed from the B-29, rather than taking off in the usual way, saved weight on fuel. The less weight the X-1 carried, the faster it was going to fly.

Awkward entry

Yeager didn't sit in the X-1 at takeoff in case it accidentally dropped from the B-29 before they reached a safe height for the rocket to fly. Near the drop zone he left the B-29's cockpit and squeezed through a narrow corridor to the bomb bay. Here he could see right down to the surface of the Earth.

The X-1 was launched in the air from a B-29 bomber to save fuel on takeoff.

Yeager had to climb down a ladder to a small metal platform and squeeze feet first through the hatch into his craft. At such a height it was viciously cold, and the wind threatened to tear his frozen fingers from the ladder's metal rungs.

Once he was inside, the door to the hatch was lowered down by his flight engineer and good friend Jack Ridley. He stood on the ladder and held it in place as it was locked from the inside. Yeager trusted Ridley with his life. Only 29, he had already established a reputation as a brilliant scientist.

"Let's go to work"

Some people said the X-1 was the most beautiful aircraft ever built. Yeager knew it was certainly the coldest. It was so chilly under the darkened bomb bay that he had to bang his gloved hands together to keep them from becoming numb. The X-1 cockpit had no heating and directly behind the seat sat several hundred gallons of freezing liquid oxygen fuel, which had coated the belly of the craft in a thin film of ice.

But now was no time to worry about the cold. "All set," radioed in Ridley, back inside the B-29's more comfortable interior. "You bet," said Yeager. "Let's go to work."

Roaring flame

The X-1 dropped like a stone. Yeager was blinded by bright sunlight and wrestled to get his

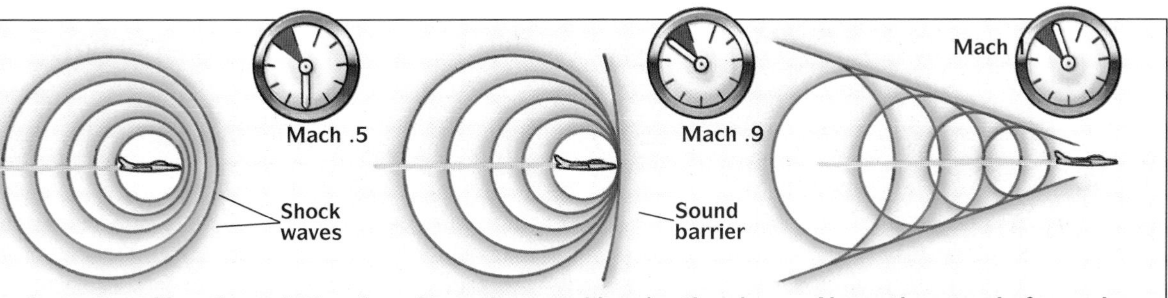

As a plane flies through the sky it creates small disturbances, or shock waves, in the air.

Near the sound barrier the plane travels at the same speed as its shock waves, causing buffeting.

Above the speed of sound a plane travels faster than the shock waves.

The Bell X-1 – bullet across the sky

The X-1 was designed to investigate the problems of flying at supersonic speed. With all four rocket chambers firing there was enough fuel for two and a half minutes' powered flight. X stood for "experimental" and only three were built.

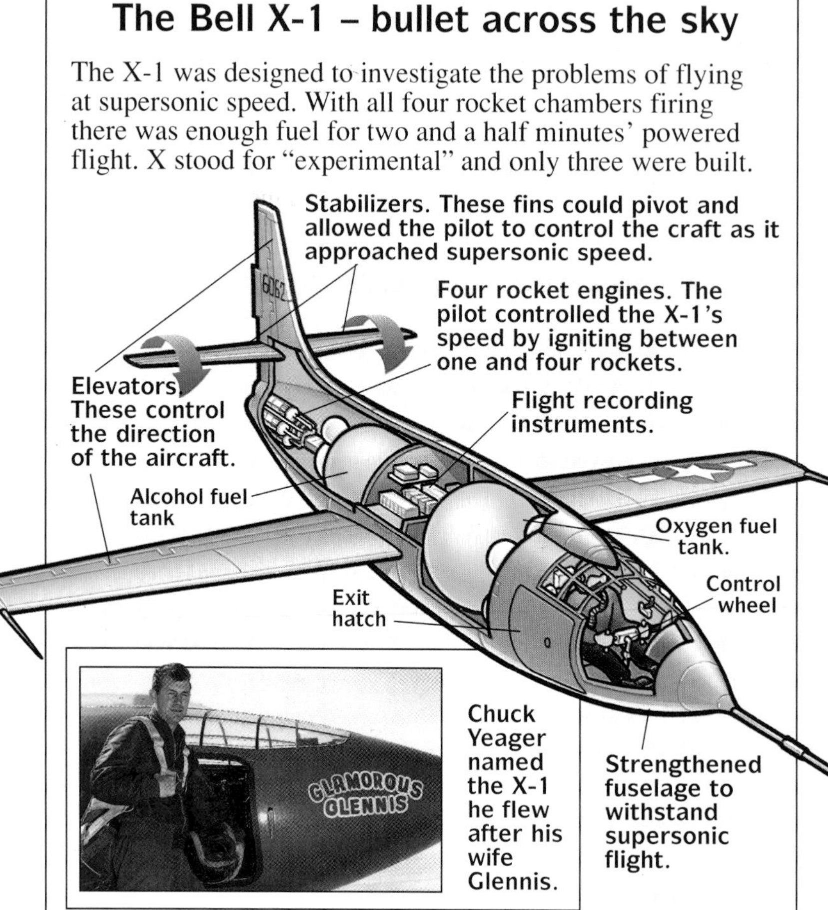

Chuck Yeager named the X-1 he flew after his wife Glennis.

craft under control. Once the X-1 was flying level he flicked the first rocket ignition switch on his instrument panel. A luminous jet of flame roared from the tail exhaust, and a huge surge of power slammed him back into his seat. It seemed as if he was heading for the very roof of the sky, to punch his way into space itself.

One by one all four engines were ignited and as Yeager reached 14,000m (45,000ft) the sky turned from bright blue to dark indigo. He was on the edge of space, flying at Mach .8.

Muroc shake-up

Down at Muroc the research engineers and airbase technicians not working on the X-1 showed little interest in the project, which they thought was doomed to failure. Experienced test pilots had been warned off volunteering for the flights. Most people thought Goodlin got out just in time.

But up on the roof of the sky the X-1 was flying beautifully. Yeager had reached maximum speed for this flight and still had half his fuel left. He thought it was time to show the Muroc personnel what his plane could do.

He cut the engines and dived toward the airbase. Lining up the rocket with the main runway he took it down to 90m (300ft) and headed for the control tower. Then Yeager hit the rocket ignition switches.

The four engines burst into life with an enormous streak of flame, making a roar that rattled every roof, window and coffee cup in the base. The X-1 shot back into the sky so fast it reached 11,000m (35,000ft) in under a minute. The fuel cut out, and Yeager glided down to the main runway, so excited he could not speak.

Everybody from Jack Ridley to his commanding officer Colonel Boyd was furious, and Yeager was seriously reprimanded . The X-1 project was one of the most dangerous series of test flights ever attempted. There was no space for fooling around.

Wheel jam

Subsequent trips proved this to be true. On his sixth powered flight on October 5, the X-1 began to be buffeted violently as Yeager reached Mach .86. Through the window he could see the rocket's wings shaking wildly.

The next flight was even worse. As Yeager pushed his jolting craft to Mach .94 he found the control wheel jammed. This was serious. At the speed of sound it was assumed that the aircraft nose would either point up or down – something which the pilot would have to correct. If he was unable to do this, the craft could spin out of control and crash.

End of the line?

Yeager returned to base sure that the X-1 project would be cancelled. Everyone agreed, apart from Jack Ridley, who quickly scribbled some calculations on a piece of scrap paper. The flight engineer explained that the reason the control wheel jammed was that at such high speed the pressure of air flowing over the rocket prevented the wing and tail elevators from moving. If this was the case, he suggested, then perhaps the aircraft could be controlled by moving the stabilizers on the tail, where air pressure was not as intense. Yeager had not done this before because he was afraid the tail might rip off, plunging the plane into a uncontrollable spin which could only end in a fiery explosion.

There was only one way to test Ridley's theory. Yeager flew back up to Mach .94, a whisker away from the speed of sound, and sure enough Ridley was right. Moving the stabilizer controls was enough to keep the X-1 flying steady, and gave Yeager the confidence to know that he would be able to keep control of his aircraft.

On target

Yeager now felt sure that he could break the sound barrier in the X-1 and survive. The next flight was planned for the following Tuesday.

On Sunday evening Yeager took his wife Glennis out riding, but disaster struck when he was thrown from his horse and fractured two ribs. The pain was intense but Yeager refused to go to the hospital at Muroc. He knew they would stop him from flying, and he was determined to finish the job.

Jack Ridley (right). His able mind saved the X-1 project from cancellation.

On Monday morning Glennis drove him to a local doctor who patched him up and told him to rest. But rest was the last thing on his mind. Despite the fact that he could do very little with his right hand Yeager drove over to Muroc and confided in Jack Ridley. He was convinced he could still make Tuesday's flight. He knew the aircraft really well now, and most of the controls would be no problem to operate.

However, lifting the handle to lock the door required a degree of strength his painful right arm did not possess. In the cramped cockpit he could not reach it with his left hand. There was a solution. Ridley found a broom and sawed off 25cm (10in). Yeager could use his good left arm to push the handle up with it. Getting down the ladder would be difficult too. Yeager jokingly suggested that Ridley could carry him piggyback.

Testing time

The B-29 took off at 8:00am on Tuesday, October 14, 1947. Officially Yeager was only meant to go to Mach .97 but, he reasoned, the more flights there were, the more chance there would be of an accident. He could be killed and the project could be cancelled. He was going to go for bust.

Getting down the ladder with two broken ribs was very painful but the broomstick worked fine. As the X-1 dropped from the bomb bay, Yeager felt perfectly in control. He ignited the rocket engines in quick succession and streaked towards the top of the sky. At Mach.88 the buffeting started and Yeager cut two of his engines and tilted the tail stabilizers. They worked perfectly. He kicked in rocket engine three again and continued to climb. The faster he went, the smoother the ride. The needle in his Mach instrument began to flutter, and then wavered off the scale.

Yeager was elated and radioed Jack Ridley in the B-29. "Hey Ridley," he giggled, "that Machmeter is acting screwy. It just went off the scale on me." "Son, you're imagining things," Ridley responded. "Must be," said Yeager in his particular slow drawl. "I'm still wearing my ears and nothing else fell off, neither."

Sonic boom

Aircraft flying faster than sound create air turbulence which causes an explosive noise called a "sonic boom", and down at Muroc a sound like distant thunder rolled over the airfield.

Only his instruments told Yeager he had broken the sound barrier. The X-1 was streaking smoothly along, and as he was flying faster than sound he did not even hear the sonic boom.

Its fuel expended, the rocket coasted down to earth, landing seven minutes later. Yeager's ribs still ached terribly, but the desert sun felt wonderful. Not since Orville and Wilbur Wright made the first powered flight in 1903 had an aircraft made such an extraordinary journey.

Terror stalks Chernobyl

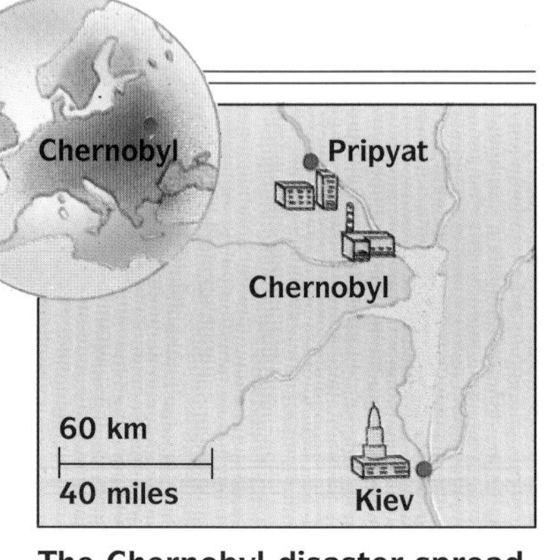

The Chernobyl disaster spread pollution (red on inset globe) over much of Northern Europe.

The towering red and white chimney of Chernobyl nuclear power station dominates the flat, swampy landscape of the Pripyat Marshes. Located 110km (70 miles) north of the Ukrainian capital of Kiev, the station had been built in the 1970s, when it was hailed as one of the Soviet Union's greatest scientific achievements.

Chief engineer Nikolai Fomin assured visitors that the chances of an explosion in this marvel of modern technology were about the same as being hit by a comet. But poor design and bad planning meant that Chernobyl was a disaster waiting to happen.

Fateful night

On the night of April 25-26, 1986, a team of engineers was carrying out tests on equipment at the number four reactor. In order to do this technicians had to slow the reactor down. Unfortunately they reduced the reactor's power so much that, like a fire about to go out, it began to shut down.

When this happens to this type of reactor it is dangerous to try to restart it. However, manager Anatoli Dyatlov, concerned that the power station would not be able to deliver enough power to nearby Kiev, ordered workers to restart the reactor.

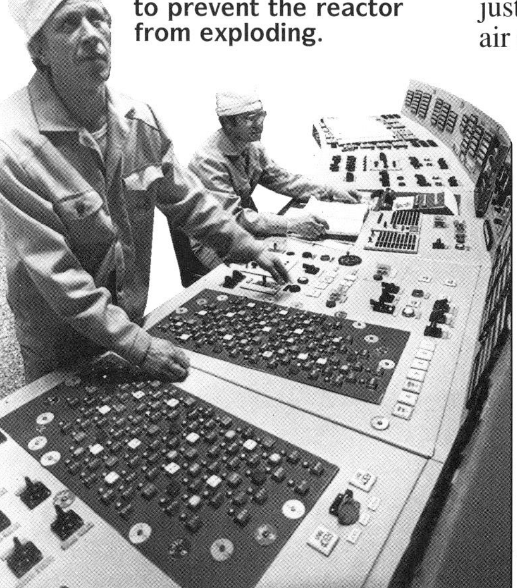

From control panels such as this, technicians tried to prevent the reactor from exploding.

Control room staff argued, but Dyatlov became enraged at their questioning his decision, and insisted they continue. In his clouded judgment he was just following procedures. An air of hysteria took hold of the control room as technicians began to grapple with tremendous forces they sensed were running out of control. They were right to feel afraid. As part of the tests the emergency water cooling system had also been cut off. The reactor began to overheat like a kettle boiling dry.

Earth shattering

In the control room technicians heard a series of ominous thumps, which made the ground tremble

Chernobyl's reactor

Nuclear power works by splitting the atoms of a metal called uranium. This creates energy in the form of heat, in a chamber known as a reactor.

At Chernobyl this process got out of hand when the reactor was slowed down and safety devices were switched off, during tests on equipment. A sudden increase in power caused the reactor to overheat and explode.

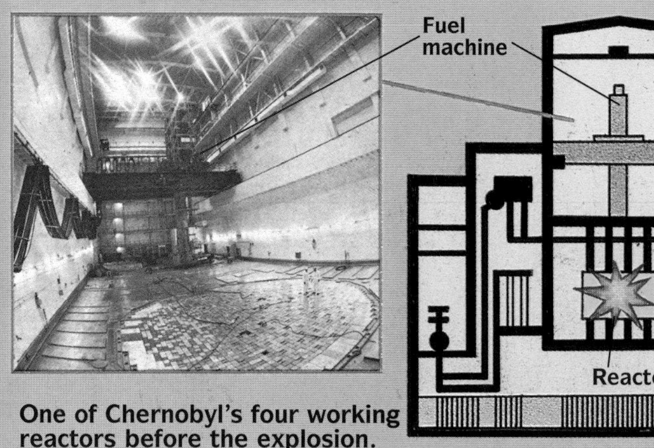

One of Chernobyl's four working reactors before the explosion.

beneath their feet. A worker rushed in with the horrific news that heavy steel covers on the reactor access points were jumping up and down in their sockets.

Then there was a huge thunderclap, the walls shook, and all the lights went out. Dust and smoke billowed in from the corridor, and the ceiling cracked open. A sharp, distinctive smell filled the air, like after a thunderstorm, only much, much stronger. It was 1:23am.

The reactor had disintegrated. It had exploded with such force that a 510 tonne (500 ton) concrete shield, which lay above it to protect power station workers from radiation, had been blown to one side. Other equipment, such as a massive fuel machine, had collapsed on top of it.

Glass and burning radioactive graphite was scattered over the reactor hall.

After the disaster radiation levels were too high for instruments to record.

Catastrophe

In the control room foreman Valeri Perevozchenko's first thoughts were for his colleague Valera Khodemchuk, whom he had last seen in the reactor hall. He dashed into the dark corridor, picking his way through clouds of dust and piles of blazing rubble, and made his way to the site of the explosion. The air seemed very thick, and he was also aware of another more sinister sensation. Deadly radiation released by the explosion was passing through him, and he could feel it burning his throat, lungs and eyes. His mouth tasted of sour apples.

Blind terror

His blood ran cold and Perevozchenko was seized by panic. He knew that his body was absorbing lethal doses of radiation, but instead of fleeing he steeled himself to stay and search for his colleague. Peering into the dark through a broken window that overlooked the reactor hall he could see only a mass of tangled wreckage.

By now he had absorbed so much radiation he felt as if his whole body was on fire. But then he remembered that there were several other men near to the explosion who might also be trapped.

Perevozchenko pressed on, running over floors that cracked with the sound of broken glass. He passed a colleague with a radiation

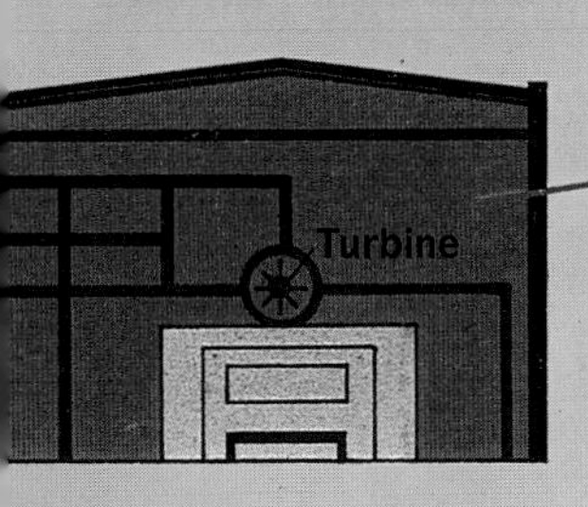

The reactor heated water into steam. The steam drove turbines which made electricity.

Chernobyl's turbine hall narrowly escaped destruction in the fire that followed the explosion.

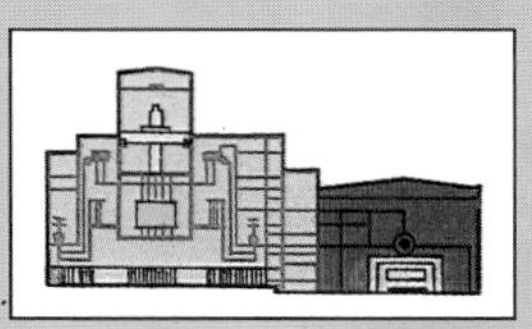

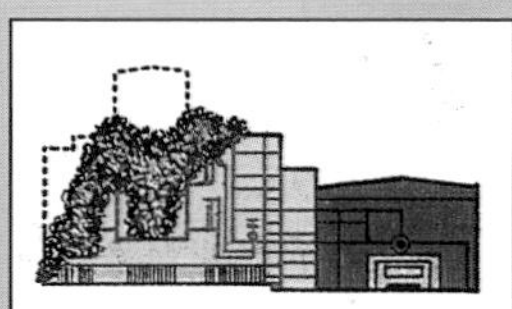

The number four reactor hall before and after the explosion.

monitoring tool, who told him one of his measuring instruments had already burned out, and the one in use was showing a reading that was completely off the scale.

Eerie shadows

Still Perevozchenko hurried on into the huge reactor hall. Looking far up to the ceiling he could dimly see that the roof had been blown off. Firemen summoned to tackle the blaze had already arrived, and their shouts rang around the huge hall. Small fires cast eerie shadows around the mangled mass of pipes and machinery. Streams of water gurgled and splattered from burst pipes. Oddest of all was the strange moaning sound of burning graphite, which was scattered around the floor. This material had come from the very heart of the reactor and was intensely radioactive.

Perevozchenko ran a flashlight over the scene and wondered what on earth he was doing in such a hellish place. Although he could not see it in the dark, the escaping radiation was rapidly turning his skin brown.

The number four reactor after the explosion.

Still he stopped to listen, in case Khodemchuk was crying for help, then shouted desperately "Valera! Valera! I've come to rescue you." The echo of his voice died away, and all he could hear was the crackle of the flames.

Ahead lay a pile of rubble, and Perevozchenko tore his hands pulling aside concrete and graphite chunks trying to make his way forward, but neither Khodemchuk nor any other colleague could be found. Exhausted, he wandered back to the control room, passing the reactor itself on the way. He could see it had been completely destroyed in the explosion and was spewing out deadly radiation rays.

Bravery in vain

Perevozchenko knew that his comrades in the control room still believed the reactor was intact, and were struggling to open water vents to try to cool it down. He also realized that the best action to take was to get as many people as possible away from the radiation.

Back in the control room Perevozchenko struggled to remain conscious. He confronted shift foreman Alexander Akimov and begged him to evacuate the building. But

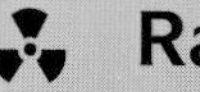 **Radiation** 

When atoms split they give off invisible rays called radiation. If people are exposed to massive doses of radiation this can cause burns and cancer.

Akimov could not believe the reactor had been destroyed. Perevozchenko's bravery had been in vain. He had been unable to rescue his colleagues, nor warn others to escape before they too became fatally affected by radiation.

Heroic actions

But other workers who courageously endangered their lives had greater success. In the aftermath of the explosion power station staff in the turbine hall were able to drain highly inflammable fuels and gases from storage tanks near to the blazing wreckage. Four received lethal doses of radiation, and another four were hospitalized with painful injuries. Had they not succeeded then even greater disaster would have struck Chernobyl. There were another three working reactors at the station, and if the fire had spread, then they also could have been destroyed.

Others too had greater success rescuing colleagues. Laboratory chief Piotr Palamarchuk, in the control room at the time of the explosion, and Nikolai Gorbachenko, also set off through the rubble to search for their colleague Vladimir

Shashenok. He had been in a room next to the reactor.

They found him quickly enough, but Shashenok was trapped by a fallen girder and had been badly burned by radiation and scalding steam. They heaved the heavy girder from his body, and carried their injured comrade to the power station infirmary. Palamarchuk and Gorbachenko had exposed themselves to heavy doses of radiation, and they too remained at the infirmary.

Older heroes

Some of the older staff at the station deliberately chose to carry out the most dangerous tasks to spare their younger colleagues. Alexander Lelechenko, the head of the electrical workshop at Chernobyl, went three times into areas of lethal radiation to disconnect dangerous electrical equipment. Standing next to piles of radioactive rubble or knee deep in contaminated water he absorbed enough radiation to kill five people. He stopped briefly to be given first aid for radiation burns, but went immediately back to work for several more hours, and only stopped when he was too ill to continue.

Firefighters

Perhaps most of all it was the courage of the Chernobyl firemen that prevented the explosion from causing even worse damage. Lieutenant Vladimir Pravik and his crew dashed to the fire moments after the explosion. Within minutes they were on the roof of the reactor hall, pouring water down on the inferno.

Almost at once the firemen began to feel sick with radiation poisoning and felt unbearably hot both inside and outside their bodies. But they all carried on fighting the fire.

The roof could collapse at any moment. The tar that lined it was melting, releasing dense toxic smoke and sticking to the firefighters' boots. Radioactive dust fell on their uniforms. One by one they began to falter. For many, fainting and vomiting spells made it impossible to continue, but due to their heroic efforts the fires caused by the explosion did not spread to Chernobyl's other reactors, and had been extinguished by dawn. The firemen paid a heavy price. Later that day 17 were taken to a Moscow hospital for specialist treatment.

By now the greatest danger was over, but the tragedy still continued to run its course. The nearby town of Pripyat, where most of the Chernobyl workers lived, was completely evacuated. 21,000 people were taken away in convoys of buses, leaving their homes and possessions, never to return. (30,000 had already fled.)

Over the next days and months firefighters and construction workers continued to work at Chernobyl. Their main task was to prevent radiation pouring out of the ruptured reactor. Helicopters flew over dropping sand on it, and eventually a huge casing was built around it.

The town of Pripyat remains abandoned to this day.

Over 100 people were taken into medical care after the first night of the disaster. Shashenok, Lelechenko, Perevozchenko and 28 others died over the next few weeks. Some lost their lives because they had tried to rescue injured colleagues. Others died because they had successfully prevented the fire spreading to the power station's other three reactors. Without their heroism Chernobyl would have faced a much greater catastrophe.

Lieutenant Pravik (far left) and his team of firefighters prevented the fire from spreading out of control. All of the men pictured here died from radiation poisoning.

The Soviet Union gave this medal to those who fought the Chernobyl fire.

Owens' Olympic triumph

To American athlete Jesse Owens, fresh off the liner *Manhatten* en route to the 1936 Berlin Olympics, the streets of Germany were quite unlike anything he had ever seen before. Most striking of all were the swastika flags that hung from almost every window or shop front. The crooked black cross on a blood-red banner was the emblem of dictator Adolf Hitler and the Nazi Party. For three years they had ruled Germany with startling brutality.

Differing views

"The important thing at the Olympic Games is not to win, but to take part," the founding father of the modern Games Pierre de Coubertin said in his speech to the Berlin spectators, "just as the most important thing about life is not to conquer, but to struggle well."

The hosts of the Games weren't convinced. Germany's Nazi party saw the whole occasion as one big advertisement for their regime and its sinister beliefs.

The Nazis believed that the German people were the "Master Race", superior human beings whose destiny it was to rule the world. Their athletes – strong, lean and usually blond – were determined to prove their supremacy in the huge 110,000 capacity Berlin Olympic Stadium.

The Nazis had strong views about other races too, especially Jewish and black people. Nazi leaders were convinced that Jews were responsible for Germany's defeat in the First World War 18 years previously, and for the country's financial collapse in the 1920s. Jewish people in Germany were subjected to daily abuse and violence. The Nazi attitude to black people was less complicated. They simply saw them as subhuman.

Boycott or not

The Nazi regime provoked disgust throughout the world, and many people felt their countries should boycott the Olympics. Aware of this disapproval the regime had softened its racist policies in the months leading up to the Olympics – for example street graffiti, billboards and political newspaper articles denouncing Jews disappeared. In the end 52 nations had agreed to attend.

As an African-American Owens too had wondered whether he should go to Berlin. But at 22 he was one of America's most promising sportsmen – a phenomenal runner and long jumper – and the Olympic Games offered him an unmissable opportunity to compete against the world's greatest athletes.

Frosty or friendly?

Owens' coach had warned him to expect racist abuse from Nazi supporters among the German people and he had come to the Olympics determined not to allow this to affect his performance. In fact the Berlin crowds were fascinated by Owens, and no sooner had he arrived in the country than he was mobbed by sports fans who had already read about his record-breaking performances.

Owens made an ideal hero. Being tall and handsome obviously helped, but the athlete had a boyish charm and modesty that made him particularly likable. As he posed for photographs and signed endless autographs he talked to the crowd in a few words of German he had taken the trouble to learn. But his

Jesse Owens powers down the track during the 100m Olympic final.

popularity proved to be just as much a problem as the expected hostility. At night Owens was kept awake by fans who came to his bedroom window to take photographs or demand autographs.

Owens won the 100m in 10.3 seconds. His victory put an end to Nazi hopes that German athletes would dominate the 1936 Games.

10 vital seconds

The Games began on August 1 with a massive celebration which glorified the Nazi regime as much as it did the Olympics. Owens' first event, the 100m, was on the day after. This brief race is one of the most glamorous and exciting in athletics, and is always the cause of tremendous interest.

Interviewed for a TV documentary twenty years later Owens described the pressure he faced in the tense moments before a race he had trained for several years to win. "When I lined up for the final...I realized that five of the world's fastest humans wanted to beat me...I saw the finishing line, and knew that 10 seconds would climax the work of eight years."

On that cold, wet afternoon the crowd held its breath, the sound of the starting pistol reverberated around the stadium, and Owens shot from the starting line. He was ahead by the first 10m (30ft). Described by one journalist as having "the grace and poise of a deer" he had a natural style that made running look easy. Sweeping to a new Olympic record and an ecstatic reception from the stadium audience, he later described the moment he was presented with his first gold medal as the happiest of his career.

In his private stadium box Nazi leader Adolf Hitler, a constant spectator of the Games, was not amused. When an aide suggested he invite Owens up to congratulate him (as he had with successful German athletes) Hitler was incensed. "Do you really think I will allow myself to be photographed shaking hands with a Negro?" he hissed.

Near disaster

The next day Owens competed in the long jump, but his three preliminary jumps nearly ended in disaster. Back home in America athletes were allowed to make a trial run up to the long jump pit as a warm-up exercise. Here in Germany the rules were different. When Owens did this and ran into the sand the judges indicated that he had failed his first jump. Badly riled, he went on to fail his second jump too. As he prepared for his vital third jump, help came from an unexpected quarter. A fellow long jump competitor named Lutz Long, who was one of Germany's star athletes, whispered a few consoling words. Encouraged, Owens jumped successfully. The competition ended with Owens jumping to victory against Long in the final. The German could not match Owens' stupendous 8.06m (26ft 5 ¼in) leap.

Long and Owens left the stadium arena arm in arm, and

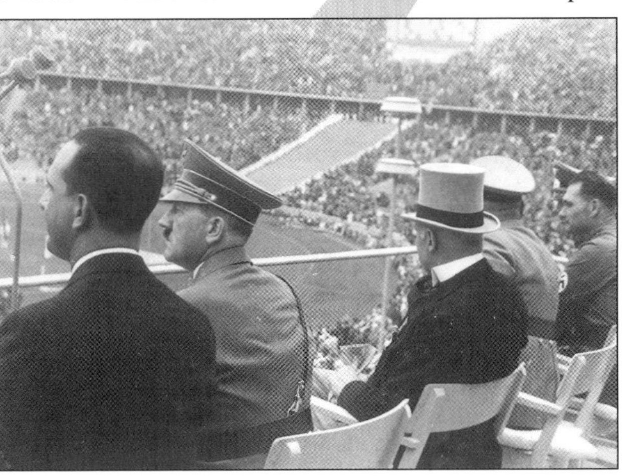

Hitler's view of the 110,000 capacity Berlin Olympic Stadium. The German dictator is second from the left.

Owens' winning jump. "I just decided I wasn't going to come down" he later told reporters. His record was only beaten in 1960.

that evening they met again at the Olympic Village and talked throughout the night. Long's blond, Germanic good looks and perfectly proportioned athlete's body were the epitome of the Nazi German racial ideal. But Long did not share his leader's racist notions. He and Owens found they had much in common. They were the same age, and from similar poor backgrounds, and both saw athletic success as a passport away from their humble origins. Long too was disturbed by the prejudice and violence he saw all around him in Germany.

More medals

There were more successes to come. On August 5 Owens took to the field to run in the 200m final. By now Nazi hopes that their athletes would sweep away all competition had evaporated. The Nazi press had started to ridicule Owens, and German officials were heard complaining about "nonhumans" being allowed to take part in the Games.

Owens refused to be intimidated by this atmosphere of petty spite, and won the 200m in a record breaking 20.7 seconds. He had a particular technique for getting off to a good start. He noticed that the starting official would make some small gesture, a flexing of the legs, or tensing of the facial muscles, just before he fired the starting pistol. From the corner of his eye Owens would watch for these signs. Forewarned, he would shoot from the starting line the instant the gun fired.

The 200m was Owens' final event, and he settled back to enjoy the rest of the Games, unencumbered by the pressure of further competition. But the US coaches had other plans for him. He was in such top form they insisted he participate in the 4 x 100m relay. (Here four athletes run 100m each, passing a baton between them.) It was an unhappy decision, which caused much ill feeling, as the coaches dropped American Jewish athlete Marty Gluckman. Owens himself protested. He'd won three gold medals already, he told the coach, and someone else should be given a chance. The coach was unmoved. "You'll do as you're told" he growled.

Another victory

So Owens once again took to the field. The American team was unbeatable. Starting the race, Owens was ahead by several paces when he passed the baton on to the second runner. Once again an Olympic record was set by the team, and Owens added a fourth medal to his collection.

It was a wonderful end to a wonderful performance, although Owens, with characteristic modesty, insisted another athlete occupy the top spot of the podium during the medals ceremony.

World famous

By now Owens was world famous, and he left Germany for a short tour of Europe, surrounded by press photographers and well-wishers.

But Hitler was deeply irritated by Owens' success. The 1936 Olympics were supposed to have been a great victory for the German Master Race. Now no one was going to forget the soft-spoken African-American who had quietly ridiculed Nazi assertions of German racial supremacy.

Owens on the winners' podium, following his long jump triumph. His friend and rival Lutz Long (right) gives the Nazi salute. Long was not a Nazi supporter, and was merely conforming with political demands.

12 seconds from death

An icy blast roared through the Skyvan transport plane as the rear door opened to the bright blue sky. On an April morning in 1991, above the flat fields of Cambridgeshire, England, three sky divers were about to make a parachute jump they would never forget.

Richard Maynard was making his first jump. He had paid £125 ($190) to plummet from 3,600m (12,000ft) strapped to Mike Smith, a skilled parachute instructor. Expecting this experience (known as a "tandem jump") to be the thrill of a lifetime, Maynard had also paid instructor Ronnie O'Brien to videotape him.

O'Brien leaped from the plane first to film Maynard and Smith's exit. The pair plunged down after him, accelerating to 290kmph (180mph) in the first 15 seconds. They soon overtook O'Brien, and Smith released a small drogue parachute to slow them down to a speed where it would be safe to open his main parachute. But here disaster struck. As the chute flew from its container the cord holding it became entangled around Smith's neck. It pulled tight, strangling him, and he lost consciousness.

Watching from 90m (300ft) above, O'Brien saw the two men spinning out of control, and when the drogue parachute failed to open he knew something had gone terribly wrong. Both men were just 45 seconds from instant obliteration.

O'Brien changed from the usual spread-eagled posture of a skydiver, and swooped down through the air toward the plummeting pair, with his legs pressed tightly together, and arms by his side. If he overshot he would have little chance of saving the two men, but this veteran of 4,000 jumps knew what he was doing.

Positioning himself in front of them he quickly realized what had happened, and tried to grab hold of Smith so he could release his main parachute. But diving at the same speed was difficult. O'Brien would be within arms length of the falling men, and then lurch out of reach. Then, suddenly, he fell way below.

Time was running out. The ground was a mere 20 seconds away, and O'Brien knew he had only one more chance. He spread his arms and legs out to slow his descent, and this time managed to connect with the pair. Whirling around and around, O'Brien searched frantically for Smith's parachute release handle.

Ronnie O'Brien

With barely 12 seconds before they hit the ground, O'Brien found the handle and the large main chute billowed out above them. Slowed by the chute, Smith and Maynard shot away as O'Brien continued to plunge down. He released his own parachute when he was safely out of the way.

By the time the tandem pair had landed Smith had recovered consciousness, but collapsed almost immediately. Only then did Maynard realize something had gone wrong. Caught up in the excitement of the jump, with adrenaline coursing through his body and the wind roaring in his ears, he had had no idea that anything out of the ordinary had happened.

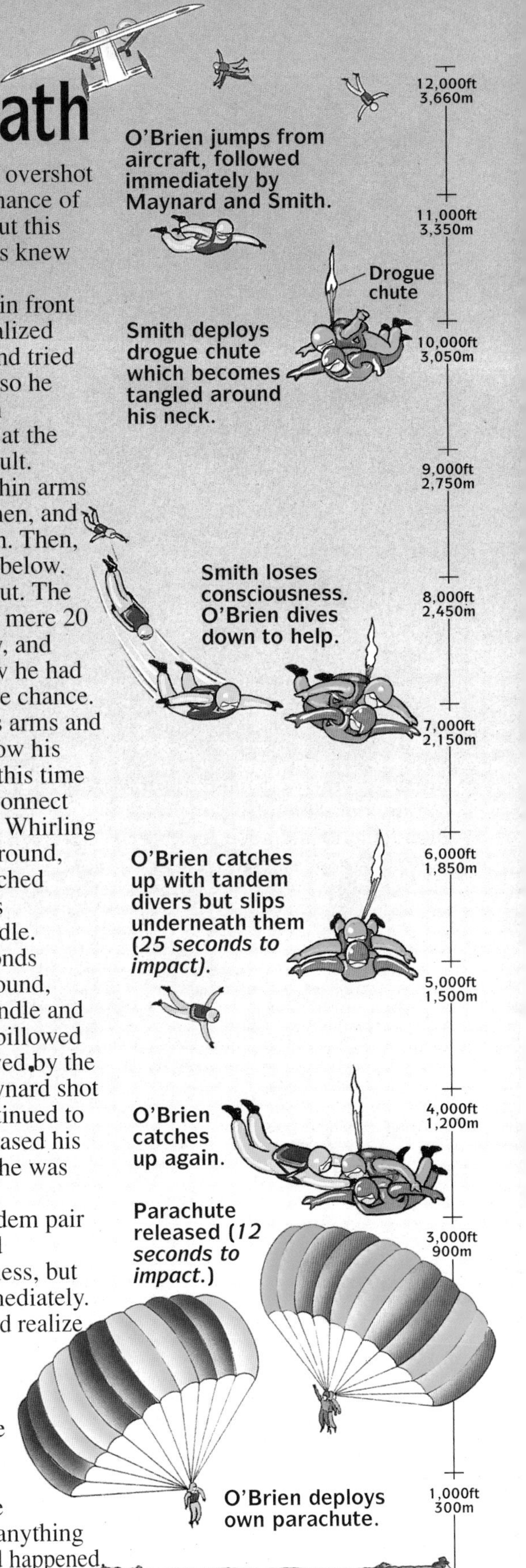

O'Brien jumps from aircraft, followed immediately by Maynard and Smith.

Drogue chute

Smith deploys drogue chute which becomes tangled around his neck.

Smith loses consciousness. O'Brien dives down to help.

O'Brien catches up with tandem divers but slips underneath them (*25 seconds to impact*).

O'Brien catches up again.

Parachute released (*12 seconds to impact*.)

O'Brien deploys own parachute.

12,000ft 3,660m
11,000ft 3,350m
10,000ft 3,050m
9,000ft 2,750m
8,000ft 2,450m
7,000ft 2,150m
6,000ft 1,850m
5,000ft 1,500m
4,000ft 1,200m
3,000ft 900m
1,000ft 300m

Geronimo's final stand

In the foothills of the Sierra Madre mountains of northern Mexico, Apache warrior Geronimo had just discovered the bodies of his wife, mother and three children. Alongside were 20 other women and children of his tribe. The year was 1850.

All had been slaughtered by Mexican soldiers while Geronimo and an Apache trading party were separated from them, bartering goods with settlers in the nearby village of Janos. The Apaches had been at war with the Mexican army for the previous two centuries. The Mexican government intended to wipe out the tribe, and had offered a reward of $100 for every Apache warrior scalp*. (Women were worth $50 and children $25.)

A terrible rage welled up inside Geronimo, but his face gave nothing away. Apache custom frowned upon open expressions of emotion. For now there were too few Apaches to retaliate, but he did not doubt his time would come.

Shortly after the massacre Geronimo had a mystical experience. Sitting alone grieving over the death of his family he heard a voice call his name. It said "No gun can ever kill you. I will take the bullets from the guns of the Mexicans... and I will guide your arrows." From that moment on Geronimo was utterly fearless in battle.

*Skin and hair from the top of the head, taken as a trophy from a dead enemy.

Direct attack

It was nine years before Geronimo was able to avenge the slaughter of his family. In 1859 he was part of a band of Apache braves (Indian warriors) led by Chief Mangus-Colorado. While skirmishing along the Mexican border at Arizpe, they came across Mexican soldiers whom Geronimo knew to be the ones who had massacred his family.

Geronimo's skill in battle was such that Mangus-Colorado gave him permission to direct an attack. Although outnumbered, Geronimo laid a careful ambush, hiding his men behind bushes in a hollow circle near to a river. As the Mexicans marched into the circle, the Indians charged.

For two terrifying hours they fought hand-to-hand. Eventually Geronimo and three other warriors stood alone on the battlefield, surrounded by broken spears, arrows and the twisted bodies of fallen men.

Geronimo in 1886. He fought so fiercely because he feared the arrival of Americans in Apache territory would lead to the demise of his people.

New threat

As Mangus-Colorado and a small group of braves looked on from a distance, two Mexican soldiers armed with rifles dashed toward the four remaining Indians. Geronimo's three comrades fell to the Mexicans' bullets, leaving him to face his assailants alone. Grabbing a spear that had fallen nearby, he hurled it at one of them and felled the man. Picking up this soldier's sword he cut down the other Mexican. Although the Indians had won

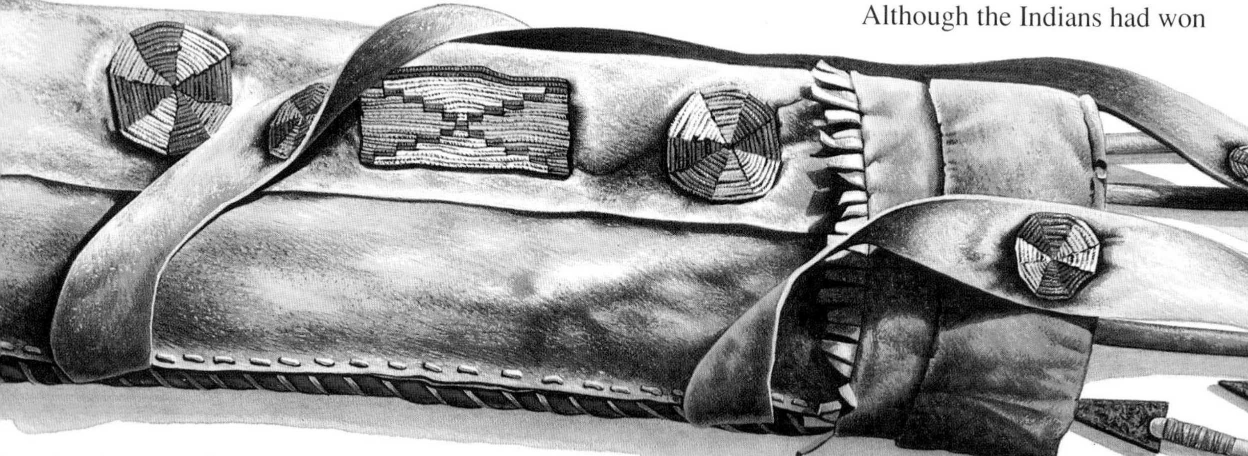

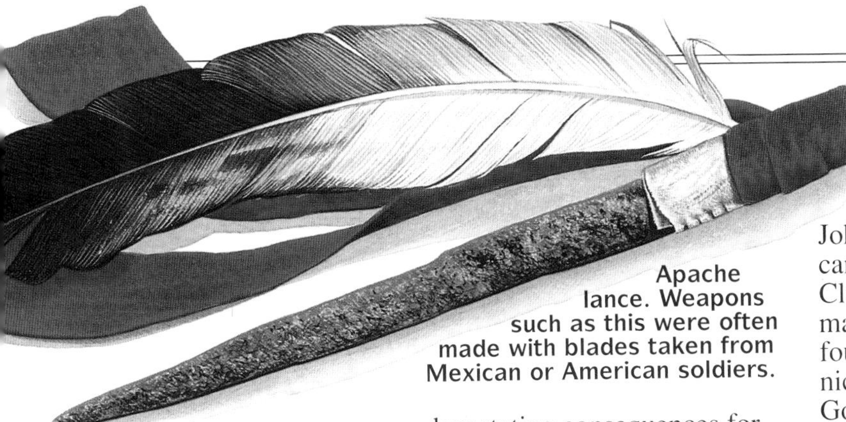

Apache lance. Weapons such as this were often made with blades taken from Mexican or American soldiers.

this battle, Geronimo was the only Apache to have fought who survived.

Commander shot

Geronimo fought scores of battles such as this, and his leadership and courage were to make him famous. On another occasion he crept up to the Mexican front line. At the exact moment their commander shouted the order for his men to charge, Geronimo shot him dead from close range. Although the ground around him was immediately peppered with gunfire, Geronimo ran for cover and escaped. Such bold actions gave great courage to his own soldiers and broke the spirit of his enemies.

The White Eyes

In the late 1850s North American settlers, dubbed "White Eyes" by the Indians, arrived in Apache territory. At first, the two cultures managed to live together, but in 1861 a series of misunderstandings sparked hostilities which would drag on for 25 years and have devastating consequences for the Apache people.

In the 1870s the United States government attempted to solve their conflict with Indian tribes by placing all Indians on "reservations". These were specific areas where particular tribes were meant to live. The government was determined not to have bands of Indians marauding around territory where American settlers were setting up farms and towns.

Reservation life

The Apache people were nomads, used to roaming their land at will, and living in one particular spot was unknown to their culture. But threatened by the American army they settled on a reservation in southeast Arizona in 1872.

This was not too great a hardship because this land was part of their traditional territory. However, in 1876 the government decided the Apaches had too much freedom and should be moved north to San Carlos, where the US Army could keep a closer watch on them. Geronimo in particular, felt strongly that they should not go. It was a fly-blown, barren stretch of desert, with little food and water to sustain his people.

A 24-year-old government agent named John Clum was appointed to carry out this resettlement. Clum had an arrogant, strutting manner, which the Apaches found irritating. They nicknamed him "Turkey Gobbler".

Although Clum managed to persuade some of the Apaches to go to San Carlos, many others looked to Geronimo to

The first Americans

Throughout the United States, from Lake Huron to Miami Beach, North Dakota to Wichita Falls, the country still bears the names of the first Americans. For three hundred years European newcomers and North American Indians waged war over possession of the land. Treaties were signed, arrangements were made, but no permanent settlement could be found. The wandering nomadic lifestyle of the Indians did not fit the European notion of towns and cities, farms and factories.

Some of the Indian chiefs believed the white man and his culture was too strong to resist, but others would not go without a struggle. The Navahos, the Cheyenne, the Sioux, the Apaches and many other tribes great and small, fought bitter battles with the American army and were massacred or imprisoned.

Apache arrow pouch and arrows. The bow was such an effective weapon that the Apaches continued to use it long after they acquired guns.

lead them away from reservation life. Over 700 joined him and fled to the hills. For three years they lived the nomadic life they were used to, gathering food where they could, and making sporadic raids in Mexico.

In 1877 Clum managed to persuade Geronimo to meet him to discuss settling in San Carlos reservation. The Indian leader and 100 Apache warriors turned up to negotiate at Warm Springs, a small town in New Mexico. But Clum had hidden 80 soldiers in the town. When Geronimo and his men arrived they were promptly surrounded. With no less than 20 rifles trained on him alone, Geronimo decided not to test his supposed invincibility to bullets, and ordered his braves to surrender.

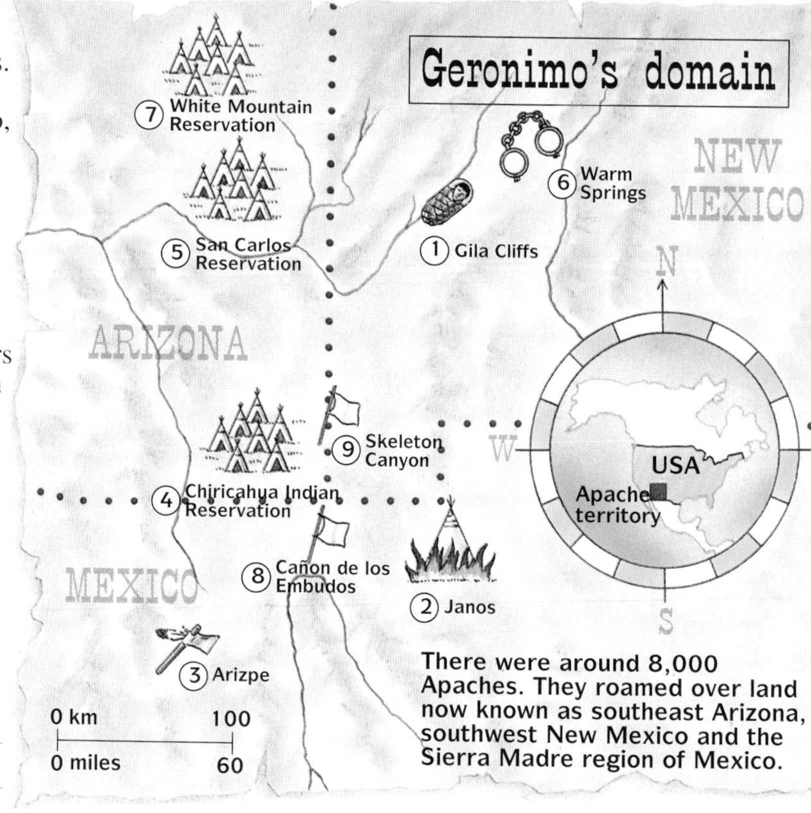

There were around 8,000 Apaches. They roamed over land now known as southeast Arizona, southwest New Mexico and the Sierra Madre region of Mexico.

Clapped in irons

Geronimo had iron shackles placed around his ankles, and he and his warriors were taken to prison. For an Apache to be caged like a wild animal was a dreadful disgrace and Geronimo must have felt a keen sense of shame, especially as his capture was the result of a simple trick.

For two months Clum tried to get government permission to have Geronimo hanged. When this was refused, Clum resigned. His successor was more sympathetic, and released the Indian leader and his fellow braves from prison.

There followed a quieter period when Geronimo and his people tried to settle at San Carlos reservation. But some American newcomers were plundering Indian goods, or trying to provoke the Apaches into violent action so they could massacre them and take their land. On top of this many Apaches were homesick, and looked to Geronimo to lead them back to their hunting grounds. So in 1882 he and a band of warriors and their families turned their back on the listless life of the reservation to roam the territories of southeast America.

Grey Wolf

The Americans were not prepared to let them be. All other Indian tribes had been defeated, and their leaders were dead or in prison. General George Crook was given the job of tracking the Apaches down.

The Apaches respected Crook, whom they called "Grey Wolf". He met with them and eventually they agreed to return with him to live on a government reservation.

Geronimo was taken to the White Mountain reservation in Arizona, and made another

Geronimo (standing, right of horse) and Apaches who had fled with him from San Carlos. 1886.

- •1823 Geronimo born here.①
- •1850 Mexican soldiers massacre Geronimo's family.②
- •1859 Geronimo avenges massacre.③
- •1872 Apaches sent to reservation in southeast Arizona. ④
- •1876 Apaches sent to San Carlos reservation. Geronimo and followers escape.⑤
- •1877 Geronimo captured by John Clum.⑥
- •1882 Geronimo leads escape from San Carlos.
- •1883 General Crook leads expedition to subdue Apaches. Geronimo sent to White Mountain, Arizona.⑦
- •1885 Geronimo leads an escape from White Mountain.
- •1886 Surrender at Cañon de los Embudos. Geronimo flees.⑧ Crook replaced by General Miles. 5,000 US troops search for Apaches.
- •1886 Geronimo surrenders to Miles at Skeleton Canyon.⑨
- •1909 Geronimo dies at Fort Sill, Oklahoma.

attempt to settle down. The American government was trying to persuade the Apaches to become farmers, but some found this life impossible to get used to. There was too little to do, so they took to drinking beer, gambling, and loafing around. For a people used to living on the land and their wits, this was no life at all.

There were other problems too. Local newspapers were calling for Geronimo to be executed, and reports reached him that American soldiers were going to kill him. So in May 1885 he rounded up 145 of his tribe, and once again fled from a government reservation.

The Apaches were masters of their terrain. They vanished among a landscape of stony mountains, pine forests and empty deserts. In this barren wasteland they knew better than anyone where to find a spring, or how to survive on mesquite beans, juniper berries and piñon nuts.

For ten months Geronimo's braves roamed the American Southwest. Terrible tales of murder and mutilation appeared in American newspapers. How much was true it is difficult to say, but any atrocities committed by the Apaches were more than matched by those carried out against them by American soldiers.

Stiffened resolve

Crook's troops pursued them relentlessly but Apaches were skilled in leaving no trail and ran rings around their pursuers. Once, Geronimo even sneaked back to the White Mountain Reservation to collect his new wife and children, right under the noses of patrolling guards. By making his enemies look foolish Geronimo stiffened the resolve of his fellow braves.

But the stresses of being constantly trailed were beginning to tell. At 62 Geronimo was an old man. In March 1886 he agreed to see General Crook to discuss surrender terms. They met in Cañon de los Embudos, just south of the Mexican border. Geronimo trusted Crook, who had great respect for the Apaches. He told him "Once I moved about like the wind. Now I surrender to you..."

Another escape

That night as the braves sat drinking whiskey, Geronimo heard again he might be hanged. Once more he fled into the Sierra Madre mountains with 34 of his followers. His escape was the final straw for General Crook. Exhausted by months of tracking such a cunning opponent, and dejected by the American Government's refusal to let him negotiate a fair settlement with his respected foes, Crook resigned.

He was replaced by General Nelson A. Miles who led an extraordinary campaign against the fugitive Apaches. Throughout Arizona and New Mexico signal teams were set up to flash Morse code messages across the country. One quarter of the entire US army (5,000 troops) were enlisted to fight 16 warriors, 12 women, and 6 children. Around 3,000 Mexican soldiers also joined the hunt. They searched in vain. Geronimo and his band had vanished into the wilderness.

Final surrender

Again, it was the strain of being constant fugitives that caused Geronimo and his group to give themselves up.

Geronimo (third from right on front row) with fellow Apache prisoners, on the way to Florida. 1886.

News also reached them that their tribe had been transported to Florida. This was a stunning blow. The Florida climate was completely unlike the arid desert terrain they were used to.

In August 1886 Geronimo met General Miles at Skeleton Canyon, Arizona, and offered his surrender. Miles's terms were reasonable. Geronimo was to be reunited with his family within five days. He would not be punished for his resistance. His tribe would once again be allowed to settle in a reservation in their Arizona homeland.

Punishment

But Miles's promises were lies. The American government had decided to punish the Apaches for their stubborn resistance. Geronimo escaped the hangman's noose by a whisker. Even American President Grover Cleveland, who had been following the Apache campaign in the newspapers, wanted Geronimo to hang.

But some justice still prevailed. The Apaches were sent to Florida, not as criminals, but as prisoners of war. For 30 years they were kept from their homeland. Although the terms of their imprisonment were light, it was not until 1913 that they were allowed to return to the more familiar territory of Mescalero Reservation in New Mexico.

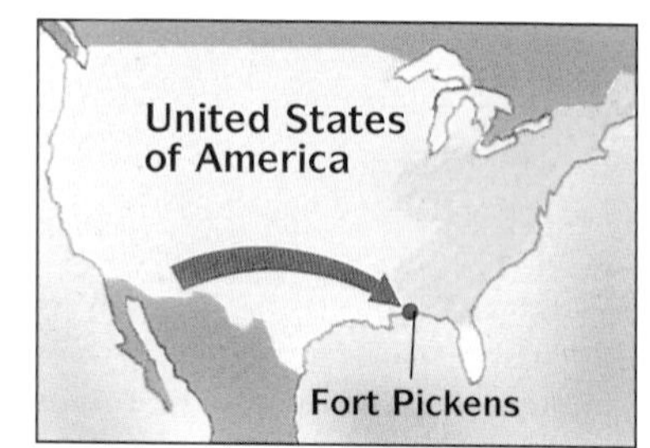

Geronimo and his Apache warriors were transported to Fort Pickens, Florida. During Geronimo's lifetime (1823-1909) the United States expanded from the green area shown here to the area it occupies today, and in many places the Indian peoples were wiped off the map.

Last great leader

In 1898, Geronimo met General Miles once again and begged to be allowed to return home. "I have been away from Arizona now twelve years," he said. "The acorn and piñon nut, the quail and wild turkey... they all miss me. They wonder where I've gone. They want me to come back." Miles was unmoved and Geronimo never saw his homeland again.

History remembers him as the last great Indian leader, and his capture marked the virtual end of Indian resistance against the American government. In defending his way of life against impossible odds Geronimo displayed a defiant heroism. He died in 1909, aged 85, and in his lifetime he had seen his tribe reduced to a quarter of their former number.

Geronimo in old age, in his garden. With him are his sixth wife and some of his children.

Brazil's rainforest hero

A soft light falls through the lush green canopy of giant trees and onto the dim forest floor. Here, a scurrying anteater rooting among the shadows is startled by a shrieking parrot, and bolts into thicker undergrowth. A butterfly, each shimmering blue wing the size of a man's hand, flutters from flower to flower.

The Brazilian rainforest in the Amazon basin is one of the most extraordinary and beautiful areas on Earth. There are so many plants and animals that scientists have only been able to identify a tiny fraction of them. Yet for much of the past twenty years this forest has been the scene of vast and ruthless devastation.

Alongside the Native American peoples who live here are some of the Amazon's more recent inhabitants – the rubber tappers. In the 1980s a tapper named Chico Mendes became a hero to millions in his struggle to save the forest from further destruction.

Remote region

Mendes was born in 1944 into a life of extreme poverty in the remote Acre (*Ak-ree*) region of the Amazon. Here there were no schools or hospitals, and only a few people could read and write. Like his father and grandfather he worked in the forest by making small cuts in rubber trees (known as tapping) to collect a fluid called latex, which is used to make rubber.

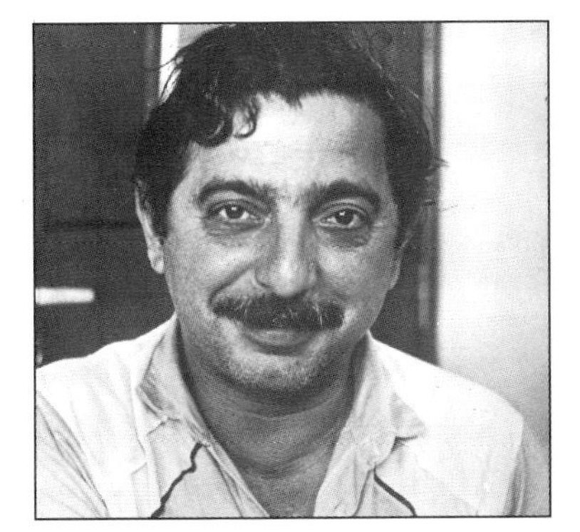

Chico Mendes in 1988.

The tappers were poorly paid by traders and landlords who treated them with great cruelty. On one occasion for example, a tapper who angered a landlord was wrapped in rubber and set on fire. Such actions went unpunished by the local police who considered the tappers to be little better than animals.

Inspiration

When he was nine, Mendes began to work as a tapper around Xapuri (*Sha-poo-rii*), a rickety riverside town deep in the Amazon forest. Residents remember him as an amiable but determined child. He was also very bright.

In his late teens he met Euclides Tavora, a local trader in his 50s with a keen interest in politics. Tavora taught Mendes to read and convinced him that the best thing the rubber tappers could do to improve their lives was to form a trade union.

During the 1960s Mendes tried unsuccessfully to do this. Most tappers were so afraid of their bosses that they accepted their grim lives with dejected apathy. But still, Mendes made many friends among his workmates, writing their letters and teaching them to read.

Changing world

The world Mendes grew up in was changing fast. When he was a child 90% of all Brazilians lived by the coast. The rest of the huge country was practically deserted. All this was to change.

In the 1950s the government decided to develop the interior of Brazil, which is mostly forest and rich in valuable minerals and metals. Over the next two decades roads were built, and businesses and landowners flocked to invest there.

Most of these landowners were ranchers raising cattle for Brazil's meat industry. Many were ruthless men who would kill anyone who stood in the way of a quick fortune.

Cattle need pasture to graze. Nearly 60% of Brazil was dense forest, and the ranchers began to tear it down to make grassland. The cheapest way to do this was to burn a huge area and then use aircraft to sow grass seeds. In this way forest could be turned into pasture in a few months, and ranchers could make quick profits.

But there was a dark side. Plants and animals were destroyed, and tappers and Native Americans who lived in the forest were driven away or murdered. As cattle fed on the land and rain washed away the soil, pasture created in this way became wasteland. After five years it was little more than desert.

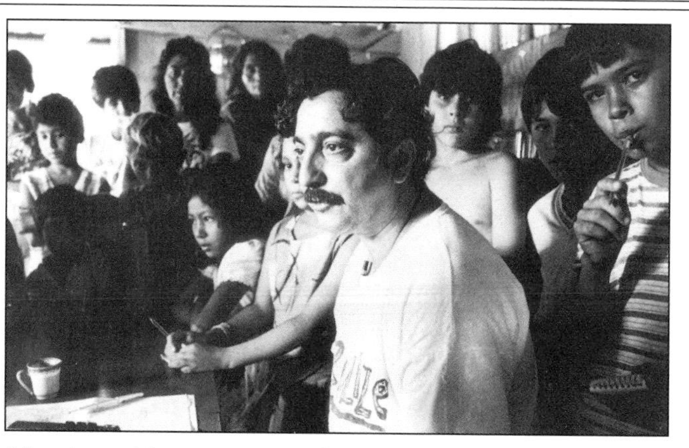

Mendes addresses a meeting of Xapuri rubber tappers.

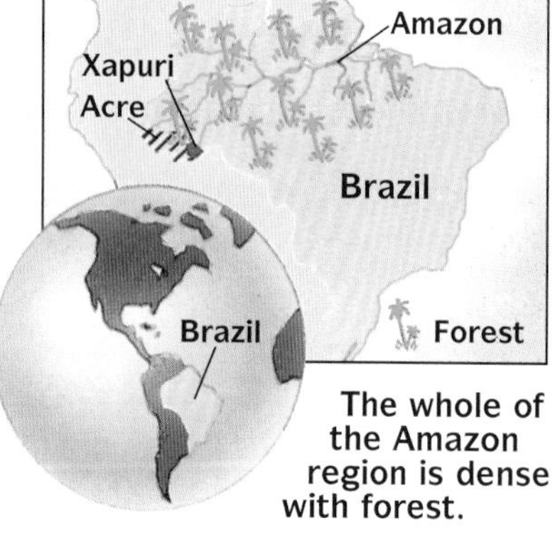

The whole of the Amazon region is dense with forest.

Acre was one of the most remote areas of Brazil. It was not until the early 1970s that ranchers lured by cheap land began to arrive there. The forest's inhabitants were treated in the usual brutal way and there was so much violence it was said that the smell of gunpowder hung in the air.

Huge areas of forest were burned to make pasture.

By then Chico Mendes had had some success organizing his workmates. He had joined forces with a tapper named Wilson Pinheiro who had set up the *Rural Workers Union*. They had come together to fight the rubber bosses for better pay, but now they were fighting against the ranchers for the very existence of the forest.

Peaceful protest

Mendes hated violence, and would not use force against his opponents. Instead, when word reached the Union that an area of forest was to be destroyed the tappers would turn up in large numbers and form a human chain to prevent ranch workers from carrying out their task. These protests did not always succeed, but large areas of Acre's forest were preserved in this way.

But Wilson Pinheiro was murdered for his resistance, and Mendes was severely beaten by hooded men in the pay of the ranchers. Death threats were a constant feature of his life, but this did not stop him becoming the president of the Xapuri branch of the *Rural Workers Union*. His warm personality brought many new recruits, and he was a talented organizer and a persuasive spokesman.

Useful friends

The feud between ranchers and union continued into the early 1980s. During this time Mendes met a Brazilian academic named Mary Allegreti. She was greatly impressed by his decency and determination, and well aware that he could be murdered at any moment.

In October 1985 Allegreti organized a conference for rubber tappers in Brazil's capital, Brasilia. The conference was also attended by conservationists and journalists from Europe and the United States. By then many people were becoming concerned about the destruction of the forest. So many trees were being burned that scientists suggested this was contributing to global warming – heating up the world's climate and causing sea levels to rise.

As well as publicizing the tappers' plight, Allegreti hoped the conference would make Mendes famous. This would make it more difficult for the ranchers to kill him discreetly.

Suspicious government

The Brazilian government was suspicious of conservationists, whom they saw as standing in the way of progress. Mendes did not want to stop the development of the Amazon, but he felt there were better ways of using it than ranching. Long term, rubber tappers and small scale farmers and nut gatherers could actually make more money for Brazil than ranchers, and also leave the forest intact for future generations. Mendes suggested that vast areas should be set aside for conservation.

Roads and Bankers

Following the conference Mendes turned his attention to another major problem. A road was being planned straight into the heart of Acre. It would only be useful to the ranchers and bring further destruction to the forest. Mendes decided to fight its construction by standing as a candidate in the government elections.

Local landowners were determined to thwart him, and bribed people to vote against him. Mendes was soundly defeated, but some good came of the campaign. His name became more widely known to Brazilian politicians and he was introduced to José Lutzenberger, a prominent Brazilian conservationist, who had close links with environmental groups in America. This was very useful. The road builders and ranchers were financed by money loaned by American banks. If American politicians and environmental groups could persuade the banks to stop lending money, this would stop further development.

Mendes decided to talk directly to them. In March 1987, wearing a suit taken from a batch of secondhand charity clothes, he visited another country for the first time in his life. Stepping into a sophisticated world of plush offices and sharp suits, Mendes was not intimidated. The businessmen and politicians he met were impressed with his keen intelligence and the reasonableness of his case. He persuaded bankers to withdraw funding for the new road until the Brazilian government took proper steps to protect the forest and its inhabitants.

Enemies within

In Acre the local ranchers were seething with rage. For years they had been able to get whatever they wanted. Now, without the new road, it would be even more difficult to expand their businesses and make more money.

One of the most ruthless Acre ranchers was Darli Alves da Silva. Darli was an unlikely looking villain – tall and thin with pipelike arms and legs, he had large glasses which perched uneasily on his bony face. Only a thin voice, which trickled out between clenched teeth, indicated that he was a dangerous man.

Determined to provoke a violent clash with Mendes and his union, Darli began to clear out tappers around the nearby town of Cachoeira (*Cash-ooo-eer-ah*), intending to turn the forest into pasture. Mendes responded with a campaign to have Cachoera declared a conservation area. Violent thugs sent by Darli interrupted protest meetings, and midnight telephone calls warned Mendes and his colleagues that they were going to be murdered.

But Mendes managed to persuade the Brazilian agricultural minister to turn Cachoeira into a conservation area – putting an end to any further destruction of the forest.

Darli was enraged with Mendes and sent his son Darci to kill him. On December 22, 1988, Mendes was shot dead as he walked into his back yard to take a shower.

"I want to live"

Shortly before he was killed Mendes said, "If a messenger came down from heaven and guaranteed that my death would strengthen our struggle, it would even be worth it." But he was doubtful. "Public rallies and big funerals won't save the Amazon," he said. "I want to live."

But he was wrong. His death caused an extraordinary outcry, catching the attention of international newspapers and TV stations. Support for his cause poured in from around the world.

His funeral was held on Christmas Day and thousands attended, including famous Brazilian politicians and entertainers. The government sent 60 policemen to hunt down his killer. Darli and Darci were arrested, and sentenced to 19 years in prison.

Mendes' funeral at Xapuri.

Perhaps the best tribute to his life came from one of the people he fought so hard to defend – a poor Brazilian rubber tapper. "They thought they killed Chico Mendes," he told a British television crew. "They didn't. Because he's alive in each of us."

Animal heroes

Snowbound rescue

New Jersey winters are harsh, and February 1983 was no exception. Unable to travel to school because of a blizzard, Andrea Andersen and her sisters were spending the day at their seaside home. Bored, they went outside to play. Her sisters soon got cold and returned to the house, but Andrea remained outside. While she was on her own, a howling gale blew her into a snowdrift right on the edge of the icy North Atlantic. Numb with cold, Andrea found that she could not get out, and shouted frantically for help. But her cries were swallowed by the swirling wind.

Next door to the Andersens lived Dick and Lynda Veit, and their Newfoundland dog Villa. Dogs have very sensitive hearing, and Villa was able to recognize Andrea's desperate cries amid the howling wind. Immediately she left the house, leapt over a 1.5m (5ft) wall and set off in search of the girl.

Villa soon found Andrea and lowered her head into the drift.

Villa with Lynda Veit and Andrea Andersen.

The helpless schoolgirl grabbed hold of the dog, who dragged her out of the snow, and then led her back to her warm home.

Goose saves guardsman's bacon

In 1837 French Canadians were rebelling against British rule in Canada, and the Coldstream Guards (a regiment of the British army) was sent by the British government to help defend Quebec. One of them was guardsman John Kemp.

One day, while on sentry duty at a farm outside the city, Kemp noticed a handsome white goose searching for food. Close by and watching intently was a hungry fox. Sensing danger the goose looked up. Both animals stood frozen as if in a trance. Then the goose panicked, and ran shrieking between the guardsman's legs. Kemp reacted instinctively, and when the fox came hurtling along, he killed it with his bayonet.

Jacob and a British soldier. The brave goose was given a gold collar by grateful guardsmen.

The grateful goose rubbed his head against Kemp's legs. From that moment on the guardsman adopted him as a pet, and christened him Jacob. It was an alliance that would save his life.

Fowl play

Shortly afterwards, Kemp was standing guard outside the farm when he was attacked by a group of rebels. As he fought for his life Jacob came squawking to the rescue, wings flapping wildly, and pecking with his sharp beak. While the distracted intruders defended themselves, Kemp grabbed the rifle that had been knocked from his hand and fired. The shot alerted soldiers nearby who came to his rescue. Jacob had saved both Kemp and his comrades. They became so attached to their unusual pet that they took him with them when the Coldstream Guards returned to London.

Jan's best friend

Few people can have had such a loyal companion, nor owed so much to their dog as Jan Bozdech of Czechoslovakia.

Shortly before the Second World War Bozdech came across a starving German Shepherd puppy. He adopted the dog, named it Antis, and the two became inseparable.

Following the German take-over of his country in 1938, Bozdech fled to France, taking Antis with him. When war broke out he became a pilot in the French Air Force and flew several missions. When France also fell to the Germans, pilot and dog left for England, where Bozdech joined the British Air Force.

After the war they returned home. But Bozdech's troubles were far from over. Czechoslovakia was now controlled by the Soviet Union, and shortly after his return a strict communist system was set up, and citizens were forbidden to leave. Bozdech had spent the last ten years fighting such tyranny and was determined to escape. With Antis and two friends he set off for Austria, the nearest non-communist country. His friends were not happy to travel with the dog, but Antis soon proved his worth, alerting them to the presence of police and border guard patrols.

During the journey the escapers had to cross a fast-flowing river under cover of darkness. Bozdech slipped, bashed his head on a boulder, and was carried away by the current. Antis bounded after him and, grabbing his master's jacket in his teeth, dragged him to the riverside. As he lay recovering, the German Shepherd trotted off to locate his two friends who had vanished into the night.

Near the border the party stopped to rest in a quiet spot, leaving the dog to keep watch. After a while a border guard appeared and began to walk directly toward the sleeping men. Antis began to bark and leap around the guard, distracting him from his route, and saved the three escapers from almost certain arrest.

Once out of Czechoslovakia, Bozdech and Antis returned to England. The dog died in 1953 and Bozdech had him buried at Ilford Animal Cemetery in London. These words are written on his gravestone:

There is an old belief
That on some solemn shore
Beyond the sphere of grief
Dear friends shall meet
once more.

Heroic homing pigeons

Pigeons are able to return home over great distances. Soldiers have long made use of this ability by employing these birds to carry messages. Some pigeons give up easily in difficult circumstances, but others are determined to return home. Pigeons have completed their missions with bullet wounds, or after being mauled by hawks. One even walked back home with a broken wing.

During the First and Second World Wars pigeons were used in great numbers and many men owed their lives to the birds. In Italy in 1943 one American carrier pigeon named G.I. Joe flew 32km (20 miles) in 20 minutes to warn a bomber squadron not to attack a village that had just been captured by American troops.

Another pigeon named Winkie was aboard a British bomber when it crashed in the North Sea. The crew survived but as no one at their base knew their position they were in danger of freezing to death. Winkie was covered in oil but this did not prevent him flying 208km (129 miles) back home with a message reporting that the plane had crashed in the sea. A search was launched and the crew's lives were saved.

A metal tube on the pigeon's leg carries a message.

Odette's ordeal

On a May day in 1943, a bedraggled French woman sat before a military court at 84 Avenue Foch, the Parisian headquarters of the German Gestapo*. She had spent a month in prison, forbidden to bathe, exercise or change her clothes. Her feet were bandaged where she had been tortured, but she still managed to project a curiously detached dignity. Her name was Odette Sansom, housewife turned British agent, and she was on trial for her life.

Odette, who spoke no German, soon became bored, and her eyes wandered around the elegantly decorated room. But when a senior officer stood up and read a statement to her, she knew proceedings had come to an end.

She shrugged wearily and told the court she did not speak German. The officer frowned and explained in halting French that she had been sentenced to death on two counts. One as a British spy, the other as a member of the French Resistance.

Odette looked on these stiff, pompous men with derision and a giggle rose inside her. "Gentlemen," she said, " you must take your pick of the counts. I can die only once."

Childhood troubles

Odette was born in Amiens, France, in 1912. Her father was killed during the First World War, when she was four. At seven she caught polio and was blinded for a year, and then spent another year with partial paralysis. These disabilities forged a fiercely independent character.

At 19 she married Englishman Roy Sansom, and moved to London. The years before the Second World War were spent raising three daughters and living the life of an English housewife.

War broke out in 1939, and in less than two years Nazi Germany had conquered almost all of Europe. The fall of France in 1940 caused Odette much grief. Cut off from her family, she worried constantly about their safety.

In the spring of 1942 Odette heard a government radio broadcast appealing for holiday snapshots of French beaches. An invasion of France from Britain was being planned, and such photos would help decide which beaches were best for landing troops. Odette had spent her childhood by the sea, so wrote to offer her help.

Secret service summons

Shortly afterward she was summoned to London. The man who met her wasn't really interested in her photographs. Instead, he asked if she would like to go to France as an agent.

She declined, but over the next week Odette wrestled with her conscience. She was torn between a deep duty she felt to France, and responsibility for her three children. Eventually she decided she would train as an agent, and found a convent boarding school for her daughters. Odette's work was so secret she could not even say what she was doing. She told them instead that she had joined the Army to work as a nurse.

British agent Odette Sansom.

So her training began. From the start the dangers were made transparently clear. "In many ways it's a beastly life" said her commanding officer Major Buckmaster. In wartime, the fate of a captured secret agent was almost always execution.

Physical fitness and self-protection training toughened her. She learned specialized skills too, such as which fields were best for aircraft to make secret landings, and how to tell the difference between German military uniforms.

Wartime France

Between 1940 and 1944 France was controlled by Nazi Germany.

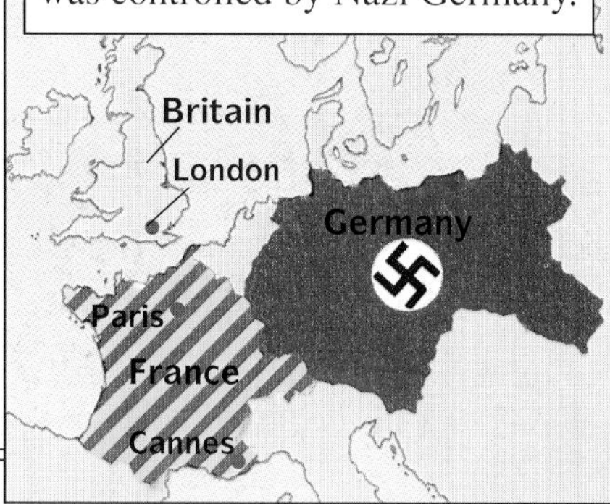

Bound for France

Her final days in England were spent making her appear as French as possible. There was a new wardrobe of authentic French clothes, her English fillings were taken out and replaced with French ones, even her wedding ring was filed off and a new French one placed on her finger.

On Odette's last meeting with Buckmaster he supplied

*Secret police

her with several different drugs – sickness pills, energy pills, sleeping pills, and most sinister of all, a brown, pea-shaped suicide pill. Buckmaster told her it would kill her in six seconds. "It's not a very pretty going-away present," he said, "so we've decided to give you another." He handed Odette a packet which contained a beautiful silver compact.

Home again

Odette was taken to France in November 1942, and began working in Cannes with a group of secret agents led by Peter Churchill, a British officer. She acted as a courier, delivering money to finance the work of the Resistance, and picking up stolen maps and documents to pass back to Britain. She found safe houses for other agents, and suitable locations for aircraft to land or drop weapons.

Churchill was impressed. His new agent was quick-thinking, and capable. She could also be very funny, and had an unstoppable determination.

Danger lurked at every turn. The Gestapo were constantly arresting Resistance workers, and anyone Odette met could be a double agent. Eventually the group was infiltrated by a traitor named Roger Bardet, who worked for the Abwehr – German Military Intelligence.

Betrayed

Churchill and Odette were seized on April 16, 1943. Even as they were bundled off at gunpoint, Odette had the presence of mind to conceal Churchill's wallet, containing radio codes and names of other agents, and managed to stuff it down the side of a car seat en route to prison.

There was no denying they were both British agents, but Odette spun a complex tale for her captors, hoping at least to save her colleague's life. She said that they were married, and Peter Churchill was related to the British Prime Minister Winston Churchill. Her "husband" was merely an amateur dabbler, who had come to France on her insistence. It was she who had led the local resistance ring, and she who should be shot. This was a convincing story and the Germans paid much less attention to Peter Churchill.

Fresnes prison

A month after their arrest they were taken to Fresnes – a huge jail on the outskirts of Paris. Odette was placed in cell 108, and a campaign to break her spirit began. Outside her door a notice read "No books. No showers. No parcels. No exercise. No privileges."

French Resistance

The Resistance were men and women who fought the Germans in France, after their country surrendered. The British secret services worked closely with them, organizing guerrilla fighters, assisting in sabotage operations, and sending back information to England.

It was here that Odette's interrogation by the Abwehr began in earnest. She also began her own campaign to survive. With a hairpin she carved a calendar on the wall and marked every day. A duct set high in the wall led to the cell below, and she was able to talk to a fellow prisoner named Michèle. This was an invaluable consolation as she was allowed no contact with other prisoners.

Gestapo summons

After two weeks the Abwehr realized their prisoner was not going to talk, and

Among many spying skills Odette learned to recognize particular German uniforms, and studied radio codes (seen here printed on a silk handkerchief that could be concealed in a wallet). Before she left for France her commanding officer gave her a silver powder compact and a suicide pill.

Odette was taken to Gestapo headquarters at 84 Avenue Foch. On her first visit she was given a large meal, but despite a ravenous hunger she only ate a little. She knew it was intended to make her sleepy and dull-witted.

Her interviewer this time was a sophisticated young man, with Nordic good looks, who smelled of cold baths and eau de Cologne. He was polite, but Odette knew she was dealing with a trained torturer. His questions about Resistance activity were met with her stock response "I have nothing to say." The interview came to an end and Odette was returned to Fresnes for the night.

Torture and tea

The next day Odette knew would be more difficult. The suave young man had run out of patience. Her stomach tightened as a shadowy assistant slipped into the room and stood menacingly behind her. First this man applied a red-hot poker to the small of her back. Still Odette would not talk. Then he removed her toenails one by one.

Throughout this torture Odette gave no cry, although she several times expected to faint. As she was asked the same set of questions she replied with the same answer "I have nothing to say."

The young man offered her a cigarette and a cup of tea. Although she was in great pain, Odette felt elated. She had kept silent and won her own victory over these inhuman thugs.

Her questioner told her they were now going to start on her fingernails, and Odette's courage wavered. But before this was done, another Gestapo man came into the cell, and told them to stop wasting their time. This was one prisoner who was not going to crack.

Back at Fresnes Odette bound her feet in strips of wet cloth and lay on her bed, sick with fear at what the Gestapo would do next. Michèle called throughout the night but she was too weak to answer.

A few days later she was summoned to the Gestapo court at Avenue Foch, and sentenced to death.

Silent good night

Returning to her cell Odette felt curiously calm. She had not betrayed her fellow agents. Many were still free and working to overthrow the Nazi regime. She bid a silent good night to each of her three daughters and fell soundly asleep. But in the early hours she woke with a start. There was no date for her execution. From now on every footstep outside her door could herald the final summons to face a firing squad.

Despite this constant threat, Odette was determined not to give up hope. Her story about being related to Prime Minister Churchill was paying dividends. Many of the prison staff who guarded Odette were intelligent enough to realize that as the war was going badly it would pay to keep on the right side of one of his "relations".

As summer turned to autumn, Odette fell gravely ill and was moved to a warmer cell. Her health improved, and in May 1944 news came that she was to be transferred to a prison in Germany. As she left, Odette caught sight of one of her interrogators and waved at him gaily, shouting "Goodbye, Goodbye." She was determined to let him know he had not broken her spirit.

The bridge of ravens

Placed on a train with an armed guard she was taken east, and spent the next few weeks in several prisons. In July of 1944 Odette arrived at Ravensbrück, a Nazi concentration camp for women. Even the name – the bridge of ravens – sounded sinister.

Within the barbed wire enclave were row upon row of decrepit huts, where guards with whips and savage dogs terrorized their skeletal, shaven-headed prisoners. Smoke from the camp crematorium filled the sky, scattering a ghastly pall of dust and ashes over the stark grey interior. The Nazis sent their enemies here to be worked to death, and every morning those

who died in the night were carried away in crude wooden handcarts. As a young girl walking the cliffs of Normandy, Odette had sometimes wondered where she would die. As she entered Ravensbrück she felt she knew the answer.

Into the bunker

The commandant of the camp, Fritz Sühren, was eager to meet Odette. She noticed how clean and well fed he looked. Like most of her captors, Sühren was interested in her connection with Winston Churchill. He ordered her to be placed in "the bunker" – the camp's own solitary confinement cells.

Commandant Fritz Sühren.

Her cell was pitch black, and for three months she was kept in total darkness. But Odette had been blind for a year of her childhood. She was used to the dark. She passed the time thinking about her three daughters, and how they had grown from babies into young girls. She decided to clothe them in her imagination, stitch by stitch, garment by garment. So completely did she fill her days deciding on the fabric, shade and style of these clothes that whenever she was visited by camp guards it seemed like an interruption, rather than the chance to make contact with other human beings.

In August southern France was invaded by French, British and American forces. This was where Odette had done most of her Resistance work. As a spiteful punishment the central heating in her cell was turned to maximum. Odette wrapped herself in a blanket soaked in cold water, but this did not stop her from becoming desperately ill. Near to death she was taken to the camp hospital. It was a strange way to treat someone who had been sentenced to execution. Perhaps the Nazis were still hoping they could break her, and she would tell them about her Resistance work.

Comfort in the dark

Away from the bunker she recovered and was returned to her cell. On the way back Odette found something that was to bring her great comfort. A single leaf had blown into the treeless camp and she scooped it into her clothing. In her dark world she would trace its spine and shape with her hands, and think about how the wind had blown a seed into the earth which had grown to a tree with leaves and branches that rustled in the wind and basked in the sunlight.

A leaf Odette found in the dusty compound of Ravensbrück brought her great comfort in the darkened bunker where she was held prisoner.

Birthday trip

On April 27 Sühren visited her. He stood at the cell door then drew a finger across his throat. "You'll leave tomorrow morning at six o'clock" he said. Odette wondered if the end had come at last. On April 28 she would be 33. Was she to die on her birthday?

That morning she could hear that chaos had overtaken the camp. Sühren arrived and bundled her into a large black van with a few other inmates. Through the window she could see the guards fleeing from the camp.

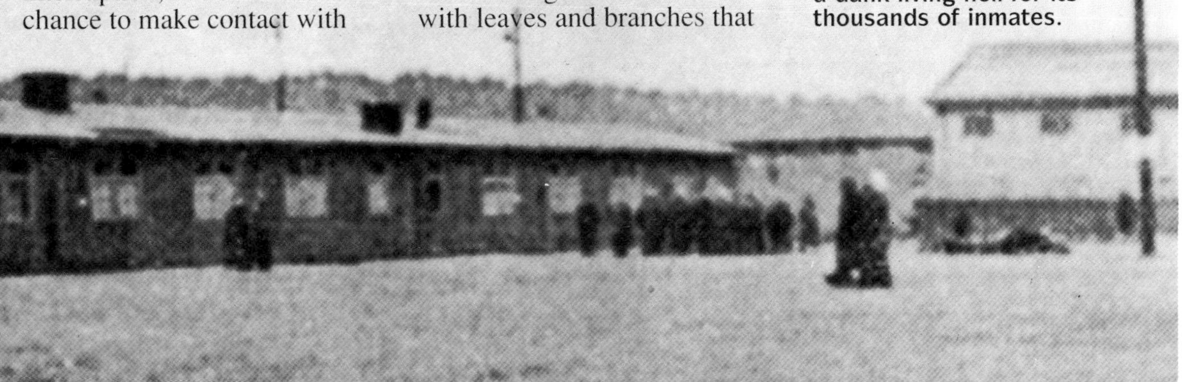

On the shore of swampy Fürstenburg Lake, Ravensbrück was a dank living hell for its thousands of inmates.

Germany collapses – May 1945

During the war the Nazis had treated Russia with appalling brutality. When victorious Russian troops swept into east Germany in early 1945, German troops were fearful of reprisals. Many fled toward British and American forces who were overrunning their country to the west, preferring to surrender to them.

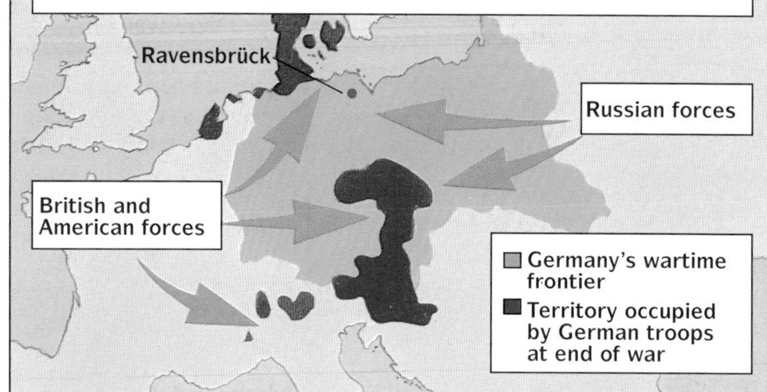

The van, together with an escort of SS* troops, drove west. It soon became clear that the war was all but over. For the next three days Sühren, his SS escort, and his small band of prisoners drove from one camp to another as Germany collapsed into anarchy.

Many prisoners, so near to freedom, but so close to death, were almost hysterical. Some whooped and screamed, making huge bonfires of anything they could find to burn. Others rushed at their guards only to be gunned down.

Sinister summons

It all seemed like a delirious nightmare. On the fourth day away from Ravensbrück a guard grabbed Odette and dragged her before Sühren. She was told not to bring her few belongings, and was certain she was to be shot. Bundled into Sühren's large staff car and with an escort of SS guards in two other cars, she sped away from the camp.

After two hours the three cars stopped by a deserted field and Sühren barked "get out". But this was not to be Odette's execution ground. Sühren offered Odette a sandwich and a glass of wine and told her he was handing her over to the Americans. At first she thought this was a cruel joke, but he seemed serious enough. Clearly he thought safely delivering Winston Churchill's relative would get him off to a good start with his captors.

At 10:00pm that night they drove into a village which had been occupied by American soldiers. Sühren marched up to an officer and said "This is Frau Churchill. She has been a prisoner. She is a relative of Winston Churchill." He handed Odette his revolver and surrendered.

Free at last

The Americans offered her a place to sleep, but Odette wanted to spend her first night of freedom out in the open. She walked over to Sühren's abandoned car and sat in the front seat feeling neither triumph nor elation, just utter exhaustion. Nearby were a party of SS soldiers, who had been part of Sühren's escort. One came over and gave her his sheepskin coat to ward off the chill of the night.

To Odette, this act of kindness by a former enemy seemed part of a strange dream, and she expected to wake at any moment and find herself back in Ravensbrück. But the dream continued. She nestled into the coat, and stared up at the stars. The village clock chimed its quarter hours throughout the night, and it was so quiet she could hear her heart beating.

Odette returned to England. Looking back on her time in France she wrote "I am a very ordinary woman, to whom the chance has been given, to see human beings at their best and at their worst."

Odette, her three daughters and Peter Churchill in London, 1946. She has just been awarded the George Cross "for courage, endurance and self sacrifice of the highest possible order."

 *Elite Nazi soldiers.

Helicopter heroes save forty

The call that came into Royal Naval Air Station Culdrose, Cornwall, UK, was desperate. In October 1989, the Pakistani container ship *Murree* was caught in a severe storm off Start Bay, Dartmouth. Her cargo had shifted in the rough weather, and tons of water were flooding into the hold.

A lifeboat had been launched from nearby Brixham, but the turbulent sea made docking all but impossible.

Sea King helicopters were despatched to help in the rescue, and within minutes two Royal Navy divers, Petty Officers Steve Wright and Dave Wallace, had been lowered aboard the heaving deck of the *Murree*.

Wright and Wallace quickly discovered that there were 40 people on board the sinking vessel, including a number of women and children. As gale force winds lashed the sloping deck they supervised the terrified crew and passengers, strapping them two at a time into harnesses, so they could be lifted into waiting helicopters. But time was running out.

Just as the last two crew members were being winched off the deck, the *Murree* lurched alarmingly as the bow sank deep beneath the waves. Wright grabbed hold of a nearby deck railing to stop himself falling. Wallace was not so lucky and slithered down the tilting deck. Catching his legs in a coil of rope, he had to struggle frantically to break free.

Moments before the *Murree* sinks a helicopter waits to rescue Wright and Wallace.

The *Murree* was going down fast. On the stern of the ship the two divers grabbed at the harness from the helicopter overhead, but it slipped from their grip. There was only one thing to do. Leaping 27m (90ft) into the boiling sea they plunged deep underwater, and surfaced to see the stern towering over them.

Fearing they would be sucked under as the ship went down, the two swam for their lives. Battered by huge waves and debris from the wreckage they floundered in the sea until a Sea King helicopter plucked them from the water.

The *Murree*'s Captain Abdul Ajeeq, who was the last crew member to leave, said "These helicopter men are fantastic. They gave us our lives". A year later Wright and Wallace's courage was officially recognized when the British government presented them with the George Medal for bravery.

Wright (left) and Wallace (right), shortly after their ordeal.

Mother Seacole's Balaclava boys

In the winter of 1855, at the height of the Crimean War, the Russian town of Balaclava could have been anyone's idea of hell. It was here that wounded or diseased soldiers from the nearby siege of Sebastopol assembled to be taken by boat to hospitals a safe distance from the fighting.

Some sat uncomplaining on hillside or horseback, their dull eyes glazed in misery. Others, with bloody bandages covering disfiguring wounds, lay on stretchers writhing in agony. Amid the chaos dying men called desperately for attention.

The Crimean War

The Crimean War (1854-56) was fought between an alliance of Britain, France and Turkey against Russia. It focused on the Crimean peninsula and a siege of the Russian city and navy base of Sebastopol.

Nurse Seacole

Along this grim procession strode an unlikely figure in a yellow dress and blue bonnet, dispensing medicine, food and encouragement. Many of the soldiers recognized this plump, middle-aged Jamaican woman. She was Mary Seacole, who ran a store and canteen close behind their front line. Some of the more delirious men took her to be their wife or mother, come to comfort them in their dying hour.

Seacole gave out medicines she had made herself, changed dressings, and gave sponge cake, broth and lemonade to the exhausted men. "They liked the cake better than anything else," she noted, "perhaps because it tasted of home." She knew that coarse army provisions were the last thing to tempt the appetite of an injured soldier.

Extraordinary life

Born in 1802 to a Jamaican hotelier and a Scottish army officer, Mary Seacole spent her childhood with British military men who she greatly admired. A brief marriage ended in her husband's death, but left her wealthy. She visited England, and Central America where she set up a string of hotels and prospected for gold.

She learned both western medicine and West Indian herbal remedies, was a skilled surgeon, and gained experience nursing cholera and yellow fever victims.

When newspaper reports of British troops suffering from cholera and typhus in the Crimea reached her in Jamaica, she was determined to help in any way she could.

Balaclava packed with ships carrying troops and supplies, 1855. The port is teeming with soldiers and traders, but no one stood still long enough to register on this early photograph.

Despite the valuable help she provided, Mary Seacole had not been welcome in the Crimea. Landing with a boat full of medicine and provisions she had been harangued by the port commander Admiral Boxer, who had recently met Florence Nightingale* and a group of British nurses. "Why are a parcel of women coming out to a place where they are not wanted?" he thundered. Boxer was only one of the hurdles Seacole had had to overcome before she could begin her work among the British troops.

Undeserved help

Although she had considerable nursing experience, her initial offer of help had been rejected by both the British War Office and Florence Nightingale's newly formed nursing organization. No explanation was given, but Seacole suspected her black skin was the reason.

Determined to help, Seacole had contacted a London relative, Thomas Day, and set up a trading company with him, intending to finance her nursing by running a store and canteen near to the battlefield. The firm of "Seacole & Day" was set up, provisions were purchased and the two had set sail for the Crimea, landing at Balaclava in early 1855.

The tribes of Balaclava

Balaclava was the main supply port for the war, and goods piled up on the quayside. There was a great deal of thieving and violence. The port was populated by Turkish, British and French soldiers, Maltese boatmen, and Greek and Italian traders – Seacole called them "the predatory tribes of Balaclava". They eyed each other suspiciously, and there were occasional outbreaks of murderous violence. With only a small band of military police to keep the peace, it was a very dangerous place to be.

For the first six weeks Seacole sold supplies from the quayside. For her protection she carried a double-barrel pistol in the belt around her waist, but confessed "I couldn't have loaded it to save my life."

Seacole at the "British Hotel". In the 1850s governments provided their soldiers with very little, and armies going into battle were always accompanied by shopkeepers selling food and clothes to those who could afford them.

She looked after the wounded whenever she could, and at night slept aboard the supply ship *Medera*. This was loaded with gunpowder, and those on board were in constant danger of instant annihilation from a fire or stray shell.

The British Hotel

After a couple of months Seacole and Day managed to build themselves a small collection of huts close to Balaclava, which they named "The British Hotel". Built from rubble it included a general store, kitchen, canteen, officer's club, store and animal pen, and accommodation for Seacole, Day and their employees.

The store claimed to sell everything from "a needle to an anchor". It was a great success and Seacole soon became well known to many of the soldiers. Aside from the warm welcome and medical

Seacole's "British Hotel" was plagued by rats.

*Nightingale was a British nurse who did much to pioneer medical treatment of soldiers during the Crimean War.

Busy day

Seacole led a hectic life throughout the war, and when it ended her health was badly affected. Her days were very much alike, except when fighting was heavy, and she was even busier. Sunday was her day of rest.

- Up at daybreak (4:00am in summer).

- Pluck poultry and prepare meats.

- Mix medicines (Seacole made her own successful remedies for cholera, yellow fever and other diseases which swept through the camps.)

- Sweep store and clean kitchen.

- 7:00-9:00am. Serve morning coffee and breakfast for troops.

- 9:30-12.00am. Attend to sick soldiers in field hospital.

- Afternoon. Run shop and canteen. (Unlike other establishments, no gambling was allowed, and only officers were permitted to drink alcohol.)

- 8:00pm. Close British Hotel.

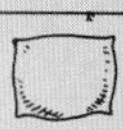
- Evening meal and sleep.

British and French soldiers pose uneasily for the camera during the Crimean War. These were the men Seacole nursed and cherished. They returned her affection, calling her "mother" or "auntie".

attention she provided, Seacole's cooking was unusually good.

Useful friends

Like many successful people Seacole had a knack for making useful friends.The Turkish leader Omar Pasha was a frequent visitor to her Hotel, and insisted she give him English lessons. He was able to learn no more than "Madame Seacole", "Good morning", and "More champagne", but he did give orders for his troops to protect Seacole's stores.

Life was still extraordinarily difficult. The Crimean winter was bitterly cold. Valuable supplies were swept away by a flash flood. On one December night 40 sheep froze to death, and thieving was a constant problem. On top of this, rats ate supplies and nibbled at sleeping hotel staff. But despite all her problems Seacole was not distracted from her work.

Front line

Seacole not only nursed soldiers at her hotel and the local field hospital, she also went out to the battlefield. Brought up among soldiers, she loved the pageantry and glamour of military life, but she was very much aware of the horrors of war.

Nursing so near the fighting required an iron nerve. Enemy fire and exploding shells still fell where she worked, and all around looters would be stripping boots and uniforms

London's *Punch* magazine made Seacole a household name during the war, and openly condemned the prejudice she had faced in trying to get to the Crimea. This illustration shows her giving out the magazine to injured soldiers.

from the dead. After heavy fighting the ground would be thick with wounded men, often horribly mutilated. Some called urgently for her attention, others, crazed with pain, tugged desperately at her clothing as she passed.

Friend or foe

Anyone who needed attention, whether friend or foe, was given it. Russian troops, some of whom had never seen a black person before, often gawped at her in astonishment, but this did not stop her caring for them. One Russian officer she helped even gave her a ring from his finger to thank her. The London *Times* correspondent William Russell mentioned her several times in his dispatches from the war. He wrote "I have seen her go down, under fire, with her little store of creature comforts for our wounded men; and a more tender or skilled hand about a wound or broken limb could not be found among our best surgeons."

Bad news

Having come to know many of the soldiers well she was constantly having to cope with news of their death. "I used to think it was like having a large family of children ill with fever," she wrote, "and dreading to hear which one had passed away in the night."

Casualties from the fighting were far outnumbered by the many soldiers dying from terrible diseases. (3,754 British soldiers fell in battle, 15,830 died of disease.) No one was safe. When cholera broke out among the troops during the summer of 1855, it even claimed the life of the British commander-in-chief Lord Raglan.

Sebastopol falls

After eleven months, the besieged Russian troops began to lose heart, and following weeks of intense bombardment, Sebastopol finally fell in September 1855. Seacole had been taking bets with her soldiers that she would be the first woman to enter the city, and she was determined to win. Borrowing two mules she loaded them with food and medicine, and set off behind the first soldiers to enter the ruins.

Seacole had done many brave deeds in her time, but this was foolhardy. True, there were wounded men to comfort, but Sebastopol immediately after the Russians had fled more than matched the horrors of the battlefield. In blazing buildings fires raged unattended and out of control. Russian positions outside the city now turned their guns on their former territory and shells fell at random.

Soldiers guzzled down stocks of Russian wine, and were soon reeling through the streets, dangerously drunk. One party of men dressed in Russian frocks and bonnets were dancing and singing among the dead and wounded. Seacole too gathered her share of souvenirs, picking up a broken bell and cracked teapot.

Rough justice

In the chaos and smoke, she soon became separated from her own soldiers, and was waylaid by a group of drunken French troops who assumed she was a Russian spy. Seacole was outraged, and knocked the hat off one of them with her broken bell. They were in no mood to argue, and she was roughly seized and dragged away to be shot. But good fortune saved her. A French officer whom she had nursed in a previous battle recognized her and ordered her instant release.

With the fall of the city the war was almost over, and troops began to leave. Although she had succeeded in her aim of nursing the soldiers, Seacole's British Hotel had become a financial disaster. Despite its success, constant thieving and the large amount of unsold goods remaining at the end of the campaign left the Jamaican nurse deep in debt.

Seacole gathered up flowers and pebbles from the graves of dead soldiers, to give to grieving relatives.

Bankrupt heroine

In the final few days before leaving she gathered flowers and pebbles from the graves of fallen soldiers who had been particularly close. These tokens she kept for herself, or passed on to the soldiers' relatives.

Seacole left the Crimea for London by steamboat, arriving bankrupt but a heroine, some months later. The very fact that she had made no profit from her hotel, when others with similar stores had made fortunes, made her even more appreciated by the British press and public. On the streets of London she was constantly stopped and thanked by soldiers who recognized her from the war. "Wherever I go" she wrote "I am sure to meet some smiling face." It was reward enough for this remarkable woman.

Stauffenberg's Secret Germany

On a spring morning in 1943 American fighter planes screamed over a Tunisian coastal road, pouring machine gun fire onto a column of German army vehicles. Fierce flames bellowed from blazing trucks and smeared the desert sky with oily black smoke. Amid the carnage lay Colonel Claus von Stauffenberg, one of Germany's most brilliant soldiers. Badly wounded, he was fighting for his life.

Best treatment

Stauffenberg was hastily transported to a Munich hospital, and given the best possible treatment. His left eye, right hand, and two fingers from his left hand had been lost in the attack. His legs were so badly damaged doctors feared he would never be able to walk again.

Willing himself back from the brink of death, Stauffenberg was determined to overcome his disabilities. He refused all painkilling drugs, and learned to dress, bathe and write with his three remaining fingers. Before the summer was over he was demanding to be returned to active service.

Hospital staff were amazed by their patient's tenacity, but it was not to fight for Nazi leader Adolf Hitler that the colonel struggled so hard to recover. What Stauffenberg had in mind was Hitler's assassination.

The *National Emblem* Nazi badge that all German soldiers were required to wear.

Murder and disaster

He had supported the Nazis once, but their murderous racism, and Hitler's decision to plunge Europe into the Second World War sickened him.

Hitler was now directing the war with startling incompetence. After one disastrous campaign Stauffenberg asked a friend "Is there no officer in Hitler's headquarters capable of taking a pistol to the beast?" Lying in his hospital bed, Stauffenberg realized he was just the man for the job.

Stauffenberg before the air attack that left him seriously disabled.

Invaluable asset

Blessed with a magnetic personality, Stauffenberg was a renowned commander. He also had a sensitive nature which invited fellow officers to confide in him. This was an invaluable asset for someone seeking allies to commit treason in the very heart of Nazi Germany.

When he recovered, Stauffenberg was appointed Chief of Staff to the Home Army. Here he became involved with General Friedrich Olbricht in a plot to dispose of Hitler and take over the German government.

Home Army hierarchy

The Home Army was a unit of the German Army made up of all soldiers stationed in Germany. It was also responsible for recruitment and training. These were its most senior commanders.

General Fromm
Commander in Chief

General Olbricht
Deputy Commander in Chief

Colonel Stauffenberg
Chief of Staff

Olbricht and Stauffenberg intended to use the Home Army to overthrow the Nazi regime. Their commander, Fromm, knew about the plot, but would neither join it, nor betray the conspirators.

Valkyrie

The Nazis had devised a plan called *Operation Valkyrie* to defend themselves against any rebellion within Germany. It worked like this: In the event of a revolt the Home Army had detailed instructions to seize control of all areas of government, and important radio and railway stations, so the revolt could be quickly put down, and prevented from spreading.

Rather than protect the Nazis, Stauffenberg and Olbricht proposed to use *Operation Valkyrie* to overthrow them. They intended to kill Hitler, and in the confusion that followed they would set *Operation Valkyrie* in motion, ordering their soldiers to arrest all Nazi leaders, and their chief supporters – the SS (regiments of fanatical Nazi soldiers) and Gestapo (secret police).

Two obstacles

There were two great obstacles to the plot. Killing Hitler would be difficult, as he was surrounded by bodyguards. Also, the head of the Home Army, General Friedrich Fromm, refused to join them. Like everyone in the armed forces he had sworn an oath of loyalty to Hitler, and had misgivings about betraying him. Fromm also feared Hitler's revenge if the plot should fail. Without Fromm's help, using *Valkyrie* to overthrow the Nazis would be considerably more difficult.

Still, the plotters were not deterred. Stauffenberg threw himself into the task of recruiting allies. He referred to the conspiracy as "Secret Germany" after a poem by German writer Stefan George, whom he greatly admired. Many officers joined him, but many more wavered. Most were disgusted with Hitler, but like Fromm they felt restrained by their oath of loyalty or feared for their lives.

Briefcase bomb

By the summer of 1944 time was running out. The Gestapo was closing in and the longer the plotters delayed, the greater the chance of being discovered.

They had decided to kill Hitler with a bomb hidden in a briefcase. Stauffenberg attended conferences with the German leader and volunteered to plant the bomb. In order to give him time to escape, the explosives would be detonated with a ten-minute fuse. This device was quite complex. To activate the bomb a small glass tube containing acid needed to be broken with a pair of pliers. The acid would eat through a thin steel wire. When this broke it would release a detonator to set off the bomb.

Stauffenberg intended to kill Hitler with a bomb hidden in a briefcase, which would be placed next to the German leader during a military conference.

Stauffenberg refused to let his disabilities affect his life. He adapted these pliers to enable him to activate the fuse on the briefcase bomb with his three remaining fingers.

Action stations

Their chance came on July 20, 1944, when Stauffenberg was summoned to Hitler's headquarters at Rastenburg, East Prussia. Together with his personal assistant Lieutenant Werner von Haeften he collected two bombs, drove to Rangsdorf airfield south of Berlin, and flew 650km (400 miles) to Rastenburg. Arriving in East Prussia at 10:15 they drove through a gloomy forest to Hitler's headquarters. Surrounded by barbed wire, minefields and checkpoints, the base – fancifully known as "The Wolf's Lair"– was a collection of concrete bunkers and wooden huts. It was here, cut off from the real world, that Hitler had retreated to wage his final battles.

Two bombs

The conference with Hitler was scheduled for 12:30. At 12:15 Stauffenberg requested permission to wash and change his shirt. It was such a hot day this seemed perfectly reasonable.

He was directed to a washroom but went instead to a waiting room and was joined by Haeften. Together they began to activate the two bombs. Stauffenberg broke the acid tube fuse on one, but as he reached for the second they were interrupted by a sergeant sent to look for Stauffenberg, who was now late for the conference.

Stauffenberg (left) with Hitler (right) at Rastenburg. The German leader thought Stauffenberg was a very glamorous figure and had a high regard for his abilities.

One bomb would have to do. But there was further bad news. Stauffenberg had hoped the meeting would be held in an underground bunker where the blast of his bomb would be lethally concentrated by windowless concrete walls. But instead he was led to a wooden hut with three large windows. The force of any explosion here would be considerably less effective.

Inside the hut the conference had begun. High ranking officers and their assistants crowded around a large oak map table, discussing the war in Russia. Stauffenberg, whose hearing had been damaged when he was wounded, asked if he could stand near to Hitler so he could hear him properly.

Hurried exit

Placing himself to Hitler's right, Stauffenberg shoved his bulging briefcase under the table to the left of a large wooden support. Just then, Field Marshal Keitel, who was one of Hitler's most adoring disciples, suggested that Stauffenberg should give his report next. With less than seven minutes before the bomb exploded he had no intention of remaining in the hut. Fortunately the discussion on the Russian front continued, and Stauffenberg excused himself from the room, saying he had to make an urgent phone call to his Berlin headquarters.

Keitel, already irritated by Stauffenberg's late arrival, became incensed that he should have the impudence to leave the conference, and attempted unsuccessfully to detain him.

There were less than five minutes to go. Stauffenberg hurried over to another hut and waited with General Erich Fellgiebel, the chief of signals at the base, and one of several Rastenburg officers who had joined the conspiracy. The seconds dragged by.

Detonation

Inside the conference room an officer named Colonel Brandt was leaning over the table to get a better look at a map. His foot caught on Stauffenberg's heavy briefcase so he picked it up and moved it to the opposite side of the heavy wooden support. Seconds later, at 12:42, the bomb detonated.

At the sound of the explosion Haeften drove up in a staff car and Stauffenberg leaped in. The two had to escape to the airfield quickly, before the "Wolf's Lair" was sealed off. The hut looked completely devastated, and as they drove away both felt confident no one inside could have survived.

Luck of the devil

They were mistaken. Brandt, and three others had been killed, but in moving the briefcase to the other side of the wooden support, Brandt had shielded Hitler from the full force of the blast. The German leader staggered out of the hut, his hair scorched and trousers in tatters. He was very much alive.

Fellgiebel watched in horror. Hitler's demise was an essential part of the plot. Still, shortly before 1:00pm he sent a message to the War Office in Berlin, confirming the bomb had exploded and ordering Olbricht to set *Valkyrie* into operation. He made no mention of Hitler's fate.

Disastrous hesitation

Olbricht, uncertain whether Hitler was dead, hesitated. Until he knew more he was not prepared to act. Meanwhile Stauffenberg, flying back to Berlin, was cut off from everything. During the two hours he was in the air, he

Wolf's Lair Conference Room

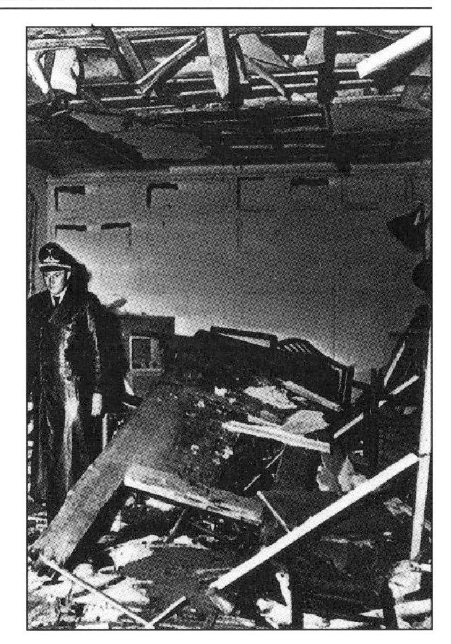

Standing next to the oak map table which saved Hitler's life, a Nazi officer inspects the devastated conference room.

expected his fellow conspirators to be engaged in a frenzy of activity. It fact, nothing was happening.

At Rastenburg it did not take long to realize who had planted the bomb. Orders were issued to arrest Stauffenberg at Rangsdorf airfield. But the order was never transmitted – the signals officer responsible for sending it was also one of the conspirators.

Only after 3:30 did the Berlin conspirators reluctantly implement their plan. Home Army officers were summoned and told that Hitler was dead, and that Operation *Valkyrie* was to be set in motion. But General Fromm was still refusing to cooperate, especially after he rang Rastenburg and was told by Field Marshal Keitel that Hitler was alive.

Stauffenberg arrives.

None the less, at 4:30 the plotters issued orders to the entire German army. Hitler, they declared, was dead. Nazi party leaders were trying to seize power for themselves. The army was to take control of the government.

Stauffenberg arrived soon afterward. He too failed to persuade Fromm to join the conspiracy. Instead the commander in chief erupted into a foaming tirade. Banging his fists on his desk Fromm demanded that the conspirators be placed under arrest and ordered Stauffenberg to shoot himself. The plotters regarded him with icy disdain, and he lunged at them, fists flailing. Subdued with a pistol pressed to his stomach, Fromm allowed himself to be locked in an office. Other officers loyal to the Nazis were also locked up. Stauffenberg now began to drive the conspirators with his usual energy and verve. For the rest of the afternoon they worked with desperate haste to implement their plan. Stauffenberg spent hours on the phone trying to persuade reluctant or wavering army commanders to support him. From Paris to Prague the army attempted to take control, and arrest all Nazi officials. In some cities such as Vienna and Paris there were remarkable successes, but in Berlin it was another story.

Not ruthless enough

The plotters were damned by their own decency. They had

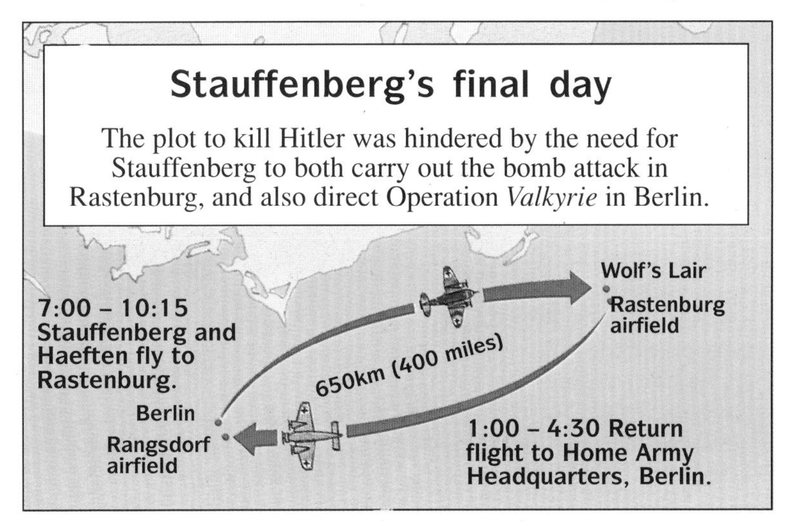

revolted against the brutality of the Nazi regime and ironically, only a similar ruthlessness could have saved them. If the conspirators had been prepared to slaughter anyone who stood in their way they may have succeeded.

They also failed to capture both the Berlin radio station, and army communication points. As the plot ground to a halt their own commands were constantly contradicted by orders transmitted by commanders loyal to the Nazis.

Surrounded

By early evening it was obvious to Stauffenberg that they had failed, yet true to his character he refused to give up. He insisted that success was just a whisker away, and he continued to encourage his fellow plotters not to give up hope. But the end was near.

The War Office was now surrounded by hostile troops, and inside the building a small group of Nazi officers had armed themselves and set out to arrest the conspirators. Shots were fired, Stauffenberg was hit in the shoulder, and Fromm was released.

Fromm's revenge

There was only one possible course of action for Fromm. Although he had refused to cooperate with the plot he had known all about it. No doubt the conspirators would confirm this – under torture or by their own free will. Fromm had to cover his tracks. He sentenced Stauffenberg, Haeften, Olbricht and his assistant Colonel Mertz von Quirnheim to immediate execution.

Stauffenberg's assistant and fellow conspirator Werner von Haeften.

Stauffenberg was bleeding badly from his wound, but seemed indifferent to his death sentence. He insisted the plot was all his doing. His fellow officers had simply been carrying out his orders.

Execution

Fromm was not convinced. The four men were hustled down the stairs to the courtyard outside. It was just after midnight. By all accounts they went calmly to their death. Lit by the dimmed headlights of a staff car, the four were shot in order of rank. Stauffenberg was second, after Olbricht. An instant before the firing squad cut him down Haeften, in a brave but pointless gesture, threw himself in front of the bullets. Stauffenberg died moments later, shouting "Long live our Secret Germany." There would have been more executions that night, had not Gestapo chief Kaltenbrunner arrived and put a stop to them. He was far more interested in seeing what could be learned from the survivors.

The remaining conspirators were arrested, but the Gestapo torturers had been cheated of their greatest prize. Stauffenberg and his fellow martyrs were buried that night in a nearby churchyard. They had failed, but with so much at stake their bravery in the face of such a slim chance of success was all the more heroic.

Keeping a secret

The plotters took great pains to avoid being discovered by the Gestapo. Documents were typed wearing gloves, so as to avoid leaving fingerprints, on a typewriter which would then be hidden in a cupboard or attic. Stauffenberg memorized and then destroyed written messages and left not a scrap of solid evidence against himself. Such was his good judgment that not a single German officer approached to join the conspiracy betrayed him.

Blackbeard meets his match

Above. Blackbeard's flag. Pirates played up their evil image for all it was worth, and the crews of many of the ships they attacked were too frightened to defend themselves.

Was there ever a villain more villainous than Edward "Blackbeard" Teach? Was there ever a calling more suited to his outsize personality than piracy? A whole head taller than most and built like a bear, Teach's nickname came from his huge black beard. Stretching down to his chest it was usually braided with bright ribbons, and obscured a face that was in constant communication with a large bottle of rum.

Teach was not without a certain roguish charm, but the succession of women who married him (14 in all) usually came to regret their decision – especially when he insisted on sharing them with his fellow pirates. He was certainly never dull company. Once, during a lull in plundering, he suggested to his crew that they make "a hell of our own" and see who could last the longest in it. He and three foolhardy competitors duly had themselves sealed into the ship's hold with several pots of blazing, foul-smelling sulphur. Teach won of course, and emerged on the deck to announce they ought to have a hanging contest – to see who could last the longest dangling from a noose.

Straight from hell

But Teach was not all fun and games. He usually went into battle with several slow-burning fuses woven into his hair. His already terrifying features cloaked in a haze of smoke, he resembled a demon from the deepest pit of hell and frightened his opponents witless.

Captured crews who had put up a fight could expect no mercy.

Below. Edward "Blackbeard" Teach. Originally a slave trader from Bristol, England, he became one of the most feared pirates in history.

The Golden Age of Piracy

The years between 1690 and 1730 have been described as the "Golden Age of Piracy". Vessels following trade routes from Europe to North and South America and Africa were regularly plundered by pirate ships, which were mainly British.

"A merry life and a short one shall be my motto" wrote pirate captain Bartholomew Roberts. The risks were great – death in battle or public execution – but the rewards were extraordinary. A successful pirate, who in everyday life might struggle to earn a pittance as a sailor, millworker or miner, could make as much in a year as a wealthy aristocrat.

Many of the merchant ships they attacked were easy pickings. Hoping to make as much profit as possible, greedy traders manned their ships with small, badly paid and badly armed crews. Faced with a horde of ruthless pirates many were not willing to defend their cargoes with their lives.

Teach even cut off the nose of one Portuguese captive and made him eat it. His own companions sometimes fared no better – he was reputed to have killed one of his crew just to remind them how evil he was.

This was all above and beyond the call of ordinary piracy, but it served its purpose. As his reputation spread, few of the merchant ships he accosted in the coastal water of North America dared to oppose him. Teach's plundered wealth also brought him friends in high places, who alerted him to the movements of government forces, and allowed him to trade his goods in coastal settlements.

Too expensive

By 1715 his activities, and those of other pirates in the Caribbean and Atlantic coast of America, were having dire economic consequences. Merchant ships were having to travel with naval escorts and the cost of insuring their cargoes became astronomical. Clearly something had to be done, but who could be found to fight such a formidable foe?

Alexander Spotswood, Governor of Virginia, put up a reward of £100 (then nearly ten years wages for an ordinary seaman), hoping to attract someone whose lust for wealth or glory outweighed his fear of this most evil of pirates. He also called in the Royal Navy, and financed a search party of two ships from his own coffers.

Maynard RN

So, on November 17, 1718, Lieutenant Robert Maynard, commander of *H.M.S. Pearl,* set sail from Virginia, together with a smaller ship *H.M.S. Lyme*. Altogether there were 60 men under his command. Maynard had been told that Teach had based himself in Ocracoke Inlet, North Carolina, and his small search party arrived there just before dusk four days later.

Maynard soon spotted Teach's ship the *Adventurer*, alongside a captured merchant vessel, and weighed anchor. He would attack the next morning. That night the pirates' drunken curses and coarse carousing drifted across the water between the two ships, and Maynard's anxious crew wondered what manner of men they would have to fight on the coming day.

Bad start

The initial attack was not promising. Ocracoke Inlet is shallow, and no sooner had Maynard's ships moved against the *Adventurer*, than they became stuck in sandbanks. Only when several heavy weights had been thrown out of the vessels were they able to proceed.

Teach watched the approaching ships with ill-tempered amusement. When the *Pearl* was close enough he called across the water,

Below. From the 1690s to 1720s piracy was rife in Caribbean and North American waters. At the time America was still a British colony, and merchant ships were defended by the British Royal Navy.

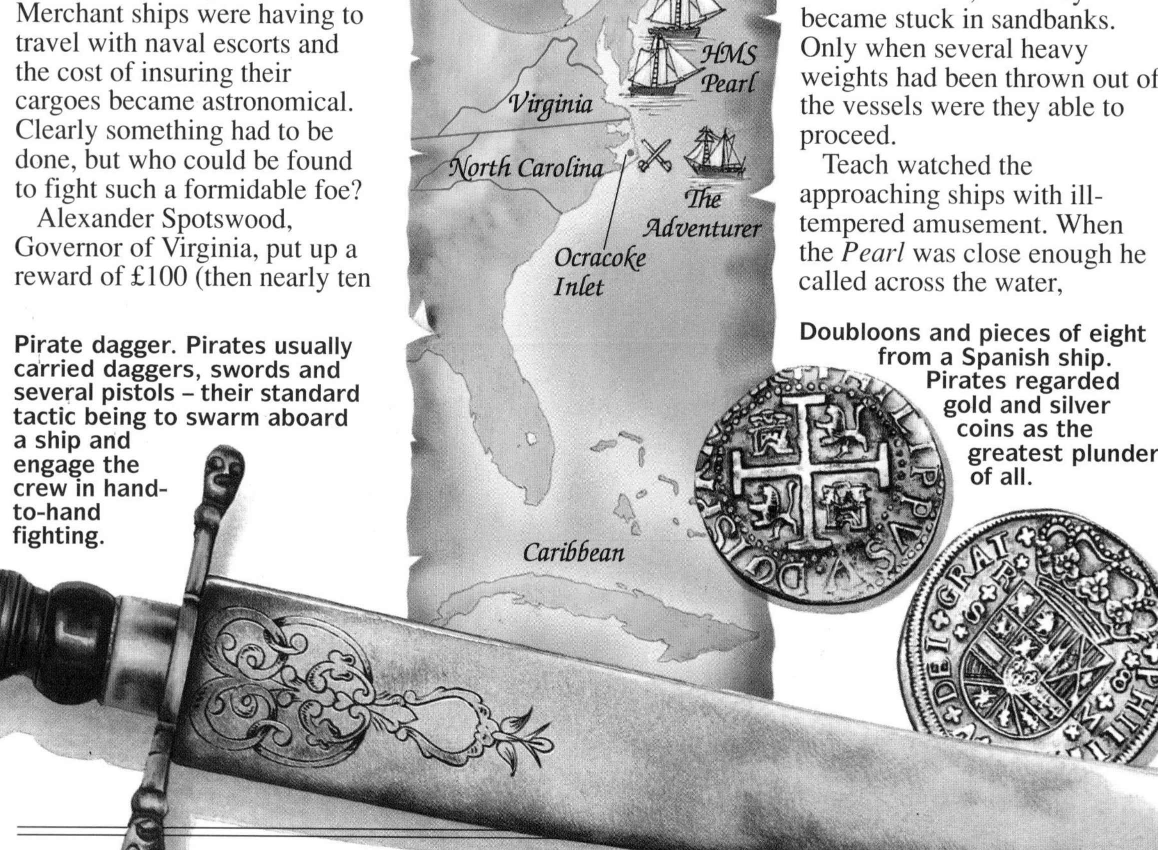

Pirate dagger. Pirates usually carried daggers, swords and several pistols – their standard tactic being to swarm aboard a ship and engage the crew in hand-to-hand fighting.

Doubloons and pieces of eight from a Spanish ship. Pirates regarded gold and silver coins as the greatest plunder of all.

demanding to know what they wanted. Maynard knew all about Teach's reputation, but was determined to inspire his frightened men with a display of bravado. "You may see we are no pirates," he called, and boldly announced he was coming to seize Teach and his crew. The despotic pirate erupted furiously. "Damnation seize my soul if I give you mercy, or take any from you," he bellowed.

Battle begins

Teach's crew were only 19 strong but they were all seasoned brigands, determined to fight to the death. As the *Adventurer* moved closer to the Navy ships it swung around and fired its cannons. *H.M.S. Lyme* caught the full force of this broadside. The captain and several of his crew were killed and the ship floundered helplessly in the water. The *Pearl* pressed on to face its foe alone.

Worse was to come. The *Adventurer*'s next volley hit the *Pearl* with similar ferocity. So intense was the fire that 21 men were injured and Maynard ordered all hands to take cover below. Teach's ship came alongside the deserted deck and his men tossed aboard blazing bottles stuffed with gunpowder, buckshot and scrap iron.

Hand-to-hand

Smoke shrouded the shattered *Pearl*, and Teach thought he had won an easy victory. His pirates swarmed aboard, but at that moment Maynard unleashed a counter attack, and lead those of his crew who could still stand out onto the deck. Bayonets flashed and pistols cracked amid the horror of hand-to-hand fighting.

Maynard fought his way toward Teach, and both men fired their pistols at point blank range. Teach's drinking got the better of him, and only Maynard found his target. But

Lieutenant Robert Maynard and Teach in combat aboard the *Pearl*. Maynard's victory marked the end of piracy in North America.

the bullet that struck the huge pirate seemed to cause him no concern, and he lunged forward with his cutlass. Maynard raised his own sword to deflect the blow, but to his horror it broke in two. Teach towered over him with a rabid leer and raised his sword to cut Maynard dead. But the blow never fell.

Saved by a seaman

One of *Pearl*'s crew, rushing to defend his captain, slashed at the pirate's throat. Yet even this was only a distraction. Spurting fountains of blood, Teach drew another pistol from his belt and aimed again at Maynard. But then a strange, faraway look came into his eyes. He swayed, and toppled over like a felled oak.

The death of the mighty Blackbeard was the turning point of the battle and the rest of the pirates were soon overcome. Ten of *Pearl*'s men lay dead, and all but one of the crew had been injured.

Poor reward

Although his victory over the fearsome Teach marked the virtual end of piracy in North America, Maynard was poorly rewarded. Alive, Blackbeard had a price of £100 on his head. Once he was dead the authorities refused to pay up. Four years of legal wrangling followed as the Navy lieutenant tried to secure a fair reward for his crew. He was eventually given £3 for his trouble, and those who fought with him were allocated half that amount.

Teach's head was cut off and hung from the *Pearl*'s bow. Such was his fearsome reputation that his body, which was thrown overboard, was reported to have swum several times around the ship in brazen defiance.

Rubble and strife in battlefield Beirut

Pauline Cutting.

A car bounced down the rubble-strewn airport road and into the suburbs of Beirut, Lebanon. Inside, insulated only slightly from the stink of open drains and dank December weather, was English surgeon Pauline Cutting. The year was 1985.

Experienced in accident and emergency work, she had been sent to Beirut by her new employers, the charity Medical Aid for Palestinians. It was turning out to be far worse than she ever expected.

Ruined city

A decade of civil war had ruined the once beautiful Mediterranean city, and 50,000 had been killed. There seemed to be no solution to the savage fighting, which flared up or died down unpredictably.

The car passed a block of bomb-damaged apartments. One side had collapsed. Crumbling concrete floors and stairways hung precariously over the road, spilling out tangled wiring and seeping streams of water. The other side of the block was still inhabited and Cutting could see people peering uneasily from cracked or broken windows.

Deeper into the bustling city the buildings closed around them, a maze of dark streets and dirty alleys. Clustered on corners were small groups of young men brandishing machine guns and grenade launchers. Occasionally the sinister silhouette of a tank could be glimpsed, skulking behind a burned-out factory, or lurking in a side street.

Chaos reigned. Here government had no control. There were no traffic signs, no policemen, no laws. Beirut was a battlefield.

Bourj al Barajneh

Cutting was taken to the Palestinian camp of Bourj al Barajneh. It was not really a camp, more a shanty town of tiny alleys.

In the middle of Bourj al Barajneh was Haifa Hospital, a five-floor concrete building where Cutting was to be in charge of the surgery

Kaleidoscope of terror

The civil war broke out in 1975, when Christian and Muslim groups fought to decide who would have the most political power. Beirut is a city of many cultures and religious views, and the situation soon became extremely complex. When Cutting arrived there were various major factions (see right), each with their own soldiers, known as *militias*.

Throughout the conflict, alliances and feuds between the militias were constantly changing. Cutting described the situation as being like a kaleidoscope, where one small twist creates a completely new pattern.

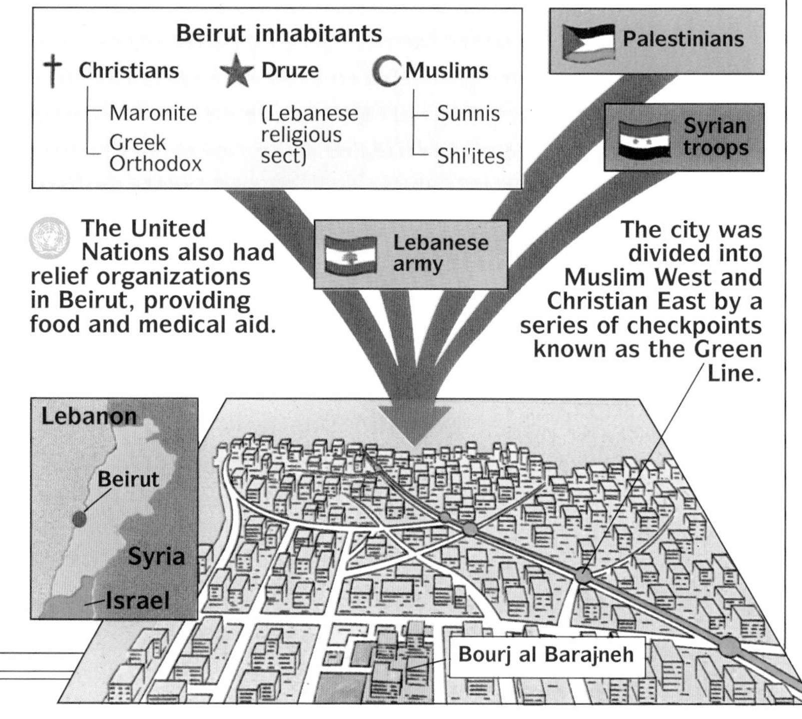

department. Like all the other buildings in the camp, it had been seriously damaged in the fighting, and the top two floors were beyond repair. The entrance hall was littered with homeless families and their belongings, and children milled around the muddy floor.

Cutting spent the first few days in a daze, wondering if coming to Beirut had been a terrible mistake. Equipment was primitive, and the staff was demoralized, but she had so much responsibility, and so much to learn there was barely time to worry about it. Most of her work involved treating day-to-day illnesses, and diseases caused by the camp's damp living conditions and dirty water. On top of this there were the casualties of the war. Cutting was used to handling terrible hospital cases such as car crash victims, and now she had to learn to deal with injuries caused by bombs, shells and bullets.

Unwanted refugees

Working in the camp Cutting learned more about the plight of the Palestinians. Driven from their homeland following the creation of the state of Israel in 1948, they lived as refugees, unwanted and in great poverty in bordering Arab states. Cutting had known little about this when she agreed to come to Beirut. After a few months at Haifa she could see the difference her work made to the lives of the people she treated, and she became determined to stay and help.

In early 1986 the situation grew worse. Violence simmered among rival groups, but most troubling of all were the kidnapping and murder of American or European residents. One United Nations worker was hanged, and his kidnappers released a video of his execution. Cutting saw the tape and was haunted by the fuzzy pictures of a hooded body swaying from a tree.

Ben Alofs

But not everything was grim. Cutting made many friends during her stay, especially a Dutch nurse named Ben Alofs, who also worked in the camp. He was tall and amiable, and was tremendously well informed about Beirut politics. Their friendship grew and one day he gave her Ernest Hemingway's *Farewell to Arms* – a novel about a passionate romance between an ambulance driver and nurse during World War One. It was something of a hint. Alofs was transferred to another part of Lebanon soon after, and left a note for Cutting saying he was falling in love with her.

Mortal danger

It was around this time that Bourj al Barajneh began to be attacked again. The camp was surrounded by Amal militia men (one of several armed Shi'ite groups) who wanted to drive the Palestinians from their city. Anyone venturing outside could be kidnapped, or killed. Inside, sniper fire and shelling became a daily danger.

On May 26, Amal soldiers stormed the camp. As the Palestinians fought to defend their territory a steady stream of injured and dying men was brought into the hospital, and Cutting and her staff struggled to save the wounded.

Haifa hospital was very poorly equipped. Many of the surgical instruments Cutting used she had brought over from England.

The next two days were just as bad, and children too were maimed in the fighting. This was Cutting's first experience of all-out battlefield surgery. Apart from the daily danger of being killed, she had to make heartbreaking decisions about who to save and who to leave to die, and cope with only the most basic supplies and equipment. There were no experts to consult, and no backup facilities, and at times she felt very alone.

Worse was to come. On May 31, as Cutting lay asleep, a shell exploded above her room. The blast hit her like a punch in the chest and thick black soot and rubble filled the hospital. The Amal soldiers attacks on Bourj al Barajneh were not succeeding, so now they subjected the camp to a week-long bombardment. During this terrifying time Cutting became close to two

Belgian doctors, Lieve Seutjens and Dirk van Duppen. They noticed how she read Ben Alofs' letter every time she lay down to sleep, and offered to teach her some Dutch, so she could speak to Ben in his own language.

At the end of June, after discussions between the warring factions, the shelling stopped. Syrian and Lebanese army soldiers surrounded the camp, to prevent more attacks by Amal soldiers.

There was other good news. Ben Alofs was back in Beirut, working in another camp. Now that Cutting was less busy she was able to spend some time with him, and also travel to England for a break.

The Camp War

She returned to the camp in late August, to be joined shortly after by Scottish nurse Susie Wighton. Another round of fighting was brewing, and the next few months were going to be extremely difficult.

At the end of October Amal soldiers attacked Bourj al Barajneh and other Palestinian camps throughout Beirut, in a campaign that became known as "The Camp War". It became impossible for Palestinians to enter or leave Bourj al Barajneh. The fighting grew fiercer, and electricity to the camp was cut off. The hospital had to rely on diesel-powered generators, and ingenious improvisation was called for. Headlight bulbs and batteries were removed from cars and rigged up to provide light in the darkened building.

The hospital became a target for the shelling. On several occasions Cutting found herself trembling with fear as direct hits shook the building to its foundations. After one near miss she was partially deaf for three weeks. One shell shattered a water tank at the top of the building and water trickled down the walls, collecting in deep pools in corridors and rooms throughout the hospital. On top of all their other troubles the hospital staff had to cope with having constantly wet feet.

By mid-November the Lebanese winter had taken hold, and in her rare moments of relaxation Cutting fantasized about sitting in front of a burning coal fire, eating stew and dumplings. Ben Alofs, braving sniper fire and shells, and loaded with supplies of cakes and custard, crept into the camp whenever he could.

As the bombardment increased, the staff moved their living quarters to the basement, sleeping in a tiny room next to the operating room. It was warmer here, and everybody was friendly, but the strain of having no privacy was difficult to endure.

One of the routes into the battered buildings of Bourj al Barajneh.

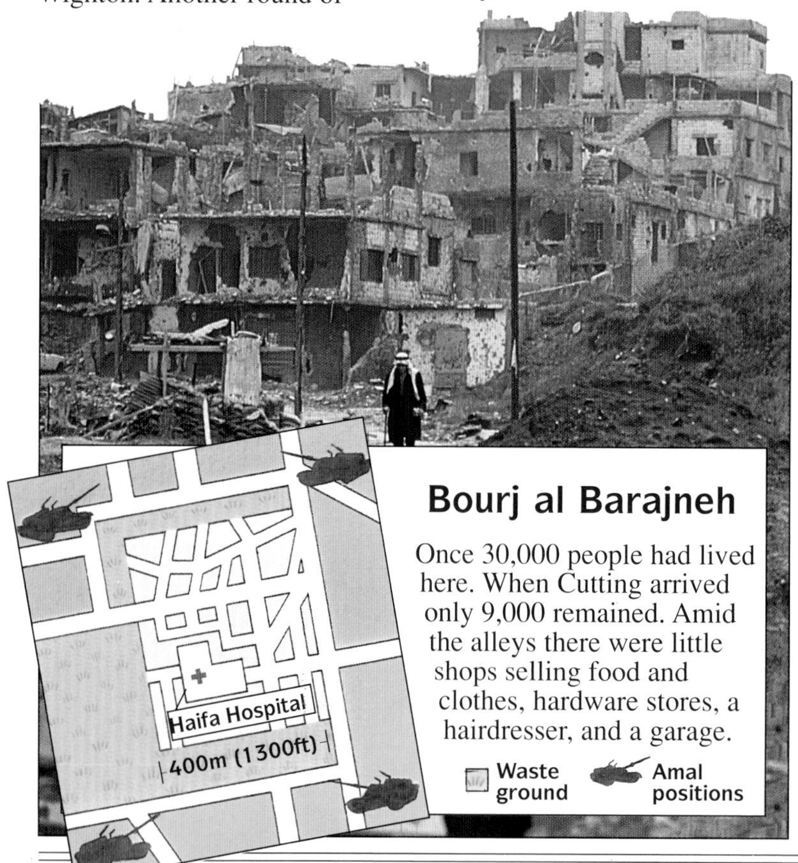

Bourj al Barajneh

Once 30,000 people had lived here. When Cutting arrived only 9,000 remained. Amid the alleys there were little shops selling food and clothes, hardware stores, a hairdresser, and a garage.

Waste ground

Amal positions

Surprising successes

Despite the hardship, hospital staff worked wonders. In November a little boy had been brought in with a terrible head wound. He was so disturbed that when anyone roused him he would cry like a cat. After a few days he started to speak, but would not open his eyes. Cutting was deeply moved by the courage children showed coping with their injuries. This boy had begun to have English lessons and every morning when she visited, he would greet her with a formal "Good morning" and say "I'm fine thank you".

He went on to make a full recovery.

On another occasion a Palestinian fighter was brought in close to death. Cutting and her team struggled all day to save him, removing 500 shell fragments from his body. He too survived. Such successes strengthened Cutting's resolve to stay in the camp until the siege was over.

When electricity to the camp was cut off, car headlights were used to illuminate the hospital.

Collapsing hospital

But the hospital was collapsing around them. Fuel was running out and the generators could only run for four hours at a time. In the cold, damp building the winter wind howled along corridors from one broken window to another, and black fungus crawled down the walls.

By the end of December the third and fourth floor had collapsed under the shelling. The drainage and sanitation system had been destroyed, everyone had lice, garbage piled up in every corridor, and rats scurried underfoot.

But there were still happy moments. January 19 was Cutting's birthday and Ben sneaked into the camp to present her with a siege survival kit – clean socks, soap, toothpaste, two candles and a packet of cigarettes. It was the best present she had ever had.

Cutting also found the people of Bourj al Barajneh were exceptionally kind. Most days a little boy would bring her food from his family. When she said he was being too generous he told her "When I have a little, I will bring you a little. When we have nothing, then I will bring you nothing."

The camp was being starved and bombarded into submission. Worst of all was the fear that if Amal soldiers did break into Bourj al Barajneh, they might massacre its inhabitants. Palestinians had been slain in their thousands when rival militias had entered other refugee camps, and Cutting began to have terrible nightmares about such killings.

It seemed that nobody was prepared to help them, so Cutting, Ben Alofs and Susan Wighton prepared a formal statement to the international media to try to draw attention to the situation in the camp. A declaration detailing the dreadful conditions of everyday life for Bourj al Barajneh's thousands of inhabitants was transmitted over the hospital two-way radio.

Identifying themselves like this took a great deal of courage. They knew the American and European media would be more interested in the siege if they knew westerners were suffering too. But this also made them a target for Amal gunmen.

The declaration was broadcast on Arab radio stations, but it caused little international interest. The situation grew worse. Starvation in the camp became so bad that the people were eating rats, dogs, cats – even grass.

Their spirits at rock bottom, Cutting and her staff radioed out another declaration calling for the siege to be lifted. This time the BBC World Service broadcast their statement.

Worst day

Friday February 13 was the worst day of the siege. A bomb

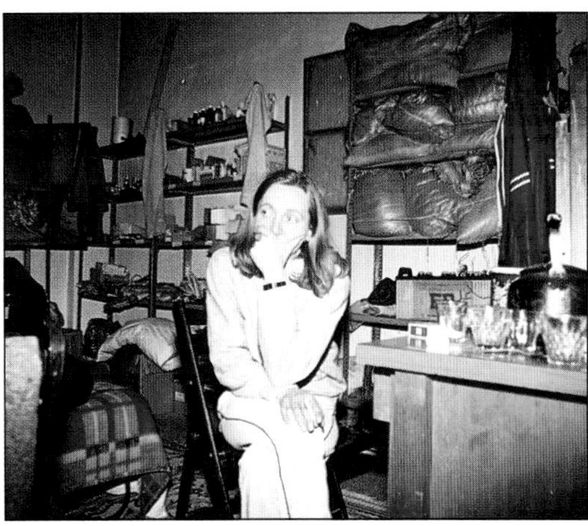

The basement operating room at Haifa. Cutting would spend at least 18 hours a day here.

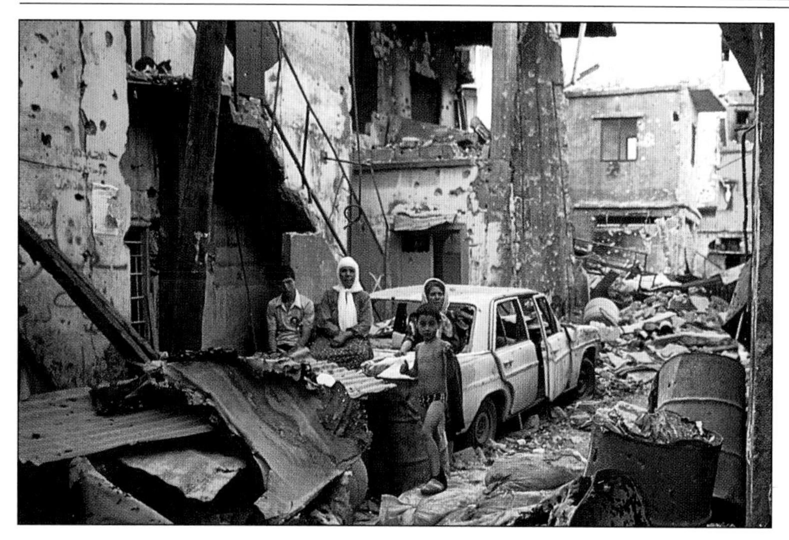

By February 1987, conditions in Bourj al Barajneh had become almost unbearable.

landed among a group of people who had ventured from their shelters and many were terribly maimed. With the barest amount of equipment and supplies the starving doctors operated on two patients at a time throughout the day.

As Cutting lay exhausted on her bed at 11:00 that night, she was roused by a message on the hospital radio. A BBC World Service reporter named Jim Muir, whose voice they all instantly recognized, was trying to contact her. Over a crackling radio link they talked about conditions in the camp, and then to Cutting's great surprise her mother and father spoke to her. The BBC had arranged a radio link up so they could talk to their daughter. Muir came back on the radio and asked if they wanted to be rescued. Cutting was determined not to leave her patients. "I'm not coming out until it's finished," she replied.

More journalists began to take an interest, and Cutting learned that other factions in Beirut were beginning to side with the Palestinians against Amal. The increasing news coverage that followed their declarations had generated some support in Beirut for the camp's inhabitants.

On February 17 a cease-fire was negotiated, and a few trucks full of food were allowed into the camp. Women were permitted to go out for a brief period each day to buy food, but they were still shot at by snipers and subjected to brutal treatment by Amal forces. "We know all about Pauline Cutting, and we are going to cut her to pieces" they told the women who passed through their checkpoints.

By now television crews and newspaper journalists were frequent visitors to the camp and the plight of Bourj al Barajneh's inmates had become a focus for the world's media. On April 8, prompted by an international outcry, Syrian troops arrived to patrol the perimeter, and for the first time in five and a half months there were no casualties admitted to the hospital. The International Red Cross arrived, along with new medical staff for the hospital. After 163 days the siege was truly over.

Home at last

It was time to go home. After many sad farewells, Pauline Cutting, Ben Alofs and Susie Wighton made their way out of the camp. Cutting was still uneasy about Amal death threats so at least 50 people surrounded her to make sure she was not seized as she left. As she got into the car she turned to look back at the camp. All the hundreds of people who had turned out to see her off were smiling and waving. It was a heartbreaking sight. She was walking away. They had nowhere else to go.

The next day they took a ferry out to Cyprus, where they were met by TV crews and journalists. All of a sudden the whole world wanted to know about these three medics from Bourj al Barajneh. In their hotel that evening they celebrated their survival with a bottle of wine and entertained themselves by turning the water and lights on and off. It seemed unreal to be somewhere where anything and everything actually worked.

Safely home and surrounded by relatives, Susie Wighton (left), Pauline Cutting (middle), and Ben Alofs (right), meet the world's press at London's Heathrow airport.

Stakhanov – Soviet Superstar

During the First World War the Russian Empire collapsed into chaos, and revolution swept away the old regime. In 1917 Russia's new rulers renamed their country the Soviet Union. They set up a communist society where citizens were supposed to have more equality and the state controlled farms and industry.

A publicity shot of Stakhanov.

Yet a decade later Russia was still very poor. Dictator Joseph Stalin, who controlled his people with an iron grip, was determined to transform his country into a powerful nation. He gave orders for huge factories, steel works and coal mines to be built. In Stalin's plan, workers on these projects, fired with patriotic zeal, would produce record levels of materials.

But most workers in these new plants and factories were peasants. In the 1920s and 30s 17 million of them moved from villages and farms to towns and industry. They were ill-disciplined and apathetic.

Execution or imprisonment was Stalin's usual method of motivating people, but on this occasion he had another tactic. If other countries made heroes of film stars or royalty, then the Soviet Union would have heroes of industry. His henchmen were dispatched to find a suitable candidate.

Stakhanov's triumph

On September 1, 1935, Soviet citizens woke to read in their morning papers that coal miner Alexei Stakhanov had dug out 104 tonnes (tons) of coal in a Donbass mine during the night shift of August 30-31. This was 14 times the amount a miner was expected to produce in a single shift. The message was clear, said the papers. If an ordinary miner could perform such superhuman work then "there are no fortresses communism cannot storm".

Stakhanov was overwhelmed with attention. He spoke on the radio, starred in newsreels, appeared in propaganda posters, and was awarded the *Order of Lenin*, the Soviet Union's most prestigious medal. He moved to Moscow where he became the figurehead for the so-called "Stakhanovite" movement, which encouraged other workers to follow his example.

Inspired by a speech

How could one man do the work of 14? Stakhanov told the Soviet people he had been inspired by a speech of Stalin's, which he heard on the radio the evening of his heroic shift. The truth was his feat was a con trick set up by the Soviet authorities. Two other miners had helped him dig the coal. A team of workers had carried it from the coalface, and done other jobs a miner would usually do himself. Stakhanov was not even an exceptional worker. He had been selected for hero status because his handsome face would look good in photographs, and he was a docile, easy going fellow, unlikely to question what he was being asked to do.

The "Stakhanovite" movement created other heroes, from steel workers to milk maids whose cows produced record levels of milk. ("Storm the 3,000 litre level" ran one slogan.) They starred in newsreels and were celebrated in biographies. "Stakhanovites" were rewarded with extra pay or smart apartments. But many were unpopular with their fellow workers, who felt their exceptional workmate showed them in a bad light. Some were attacked or even murdered.

And what of Stakhanov himself? The Soviet superman who swapped the Donbass coal fields for a desk in Moscow proved to be a poor organizer. When other workplace heroes sprang up to replace him he was quietly dropped from his post, and vanished into obscurity.

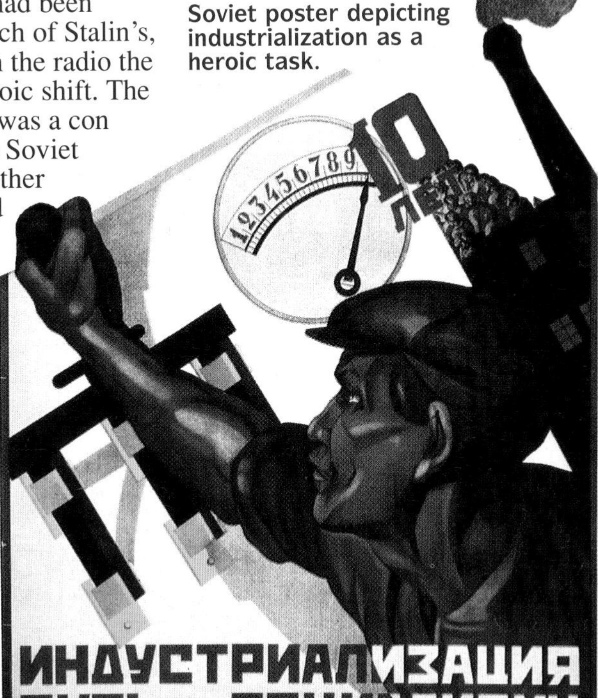

Soviet poster depicting industrialization as a heroic task.

Cosmonaut number one

Outer space; an airless, endless realm, host to lethal radiation, meteor storms, and perils unknown to science. Devoid of life and unimaginably bleak.

In the dead of night, April 12, 1961, on a windswept plain in the central Soviet Union, a towering green rocket named *Vostok 1* sat pointing at the sky. Its task, to hurl a man up into the deadly environment of space.

Technicians swarmed around the concrete launch pad and huge steel gantries that connected and supported a mass of electricity cables and fuel pipes. These snaked into the thin metal casing of the rocket, which creaked and groaned as liquid oxygen boiled away from access vents and into the cold night air.

Capsule to space

As the first rays of the sun caught on the rocket's pointed tip, a small bus drew up beside it. Several figures emerged, including one dressed in a hefty orange protective suit and a large spherical helmet. The technicians paused from their work as this man made a brief speech, raising his hands to acknowledge their applause.

Then he boarded a platform which took him to a small instrument-packed capsule at the top of the rocket. Here he was strapped into a couch, and 30 nuts were screwed in around an exit hatch to seal him in. One by one the technicians retired to the safety of nearby concrete bunkers, leaving him alone with his thoughts. The waiting began.

The man cocooned in this tiny capsule was former jet fighter pilot Yuri Gagarin, the Soviet Union's designated "Cosmonaut* number one". The amiable 27-year-old son of a carpenter and dairy maid had been selected from over 3,000 volunteers to be the first man in space. No one on the project doubted he was the best person for the job – a cool and clear thinker, with great stamina and personal courage. If anyone could survive the dangers of space it was Gagarin.

Like the great seafarers who first explored the world's oceans three centuries before, he was venturing into the unknown. They had feared storms, sea monsters or savage tribes. The fears Gagarin faced were far stranger.

Weightless puzzle

The extreme environment of space was complicated by the phenomenon of weightlessness. On Earth gravity holds everything in its place. In space it does not exist.

***Vostok 1* thunders into space, April 12, 1961.**

Yuri Gagarin, the first man in space. This photo of him in a jet pilot uniform became a popular Soviet pin-up.

Although animals had been sent into orbit and lived, many scientists still wondered whether a man would be able to survive without gravity. Would blood still flow around his body? Would he choke on food? Worst of all, would his mind become so disoriented by this alien sensation that it would cease to function? (At the time it was a commonly held fear that space voyagers could return from space as burned out zombies.)

Big bang

There were other more obvious worries. A space voyager would travel at speeds no human had experienced before. The physical damage this might cause could only be guessed at. Most importantly, the business of sending a vehicle into orbit by igniting thousands of tons of highly volatile, explosive fuel was never going to make space travel a particularly safe activity. In 1961 rocket science was in its infancy, and the seven months prior to Gagarin's flight had seen some terrible disasters.

One rocket, aimed at the planet Mars, had blown up on

*The Russians called their spacemen cosmonauts. (From Cosmos meaning the universe, and nautes, a Greek word for sailor.)

the launch pad, killing the Soviet's space project director Marshall Mitrofan Nedelin, and scores of his best technicians. More ominously still, several unmanned flights in the *Vostok*-type craft that Gagarin now occupied had ended with the capsule locked in an eternal orbit, or burning up on its return to Earth.

Cold War

The world Gagarin was about to leave had settled into an uneasy peace following World War Two, which had ended 16 years before. Its two principal victors – the United States and the Soviet Union – were now hostile rivals. Each side taunted the other, stopping just short of coming to blows, and vied with the other to demonstrate their superiority to the watching world. Space had become the new front line for this contest, and there was intense competition to see who would be the first to put a man into orbit.

Blast off

For three hours Gagarin sat waiting, as rocket engineers ran through final checks. Then, at seven minutes past nine, it was time to go. Four metal gantries which supported the rocket unfolded, its engines ignited and *Vostok 1* rose slowly into the air. In his capsule Gagarin heard a shrill whistle and then a mighty roar. As the rocket built up speed he was pressed hard into his seat. After a minute the acceleration was so great he could barely move. Technicians monitoring his physical reactions noted his heart rate rise from its usual 64 beats a minute to 150.

Gagarin's pioneering spacecraft

Vostok 1 had two sections. Only the spherical upper module containing the cosmonaut came back to Earth.

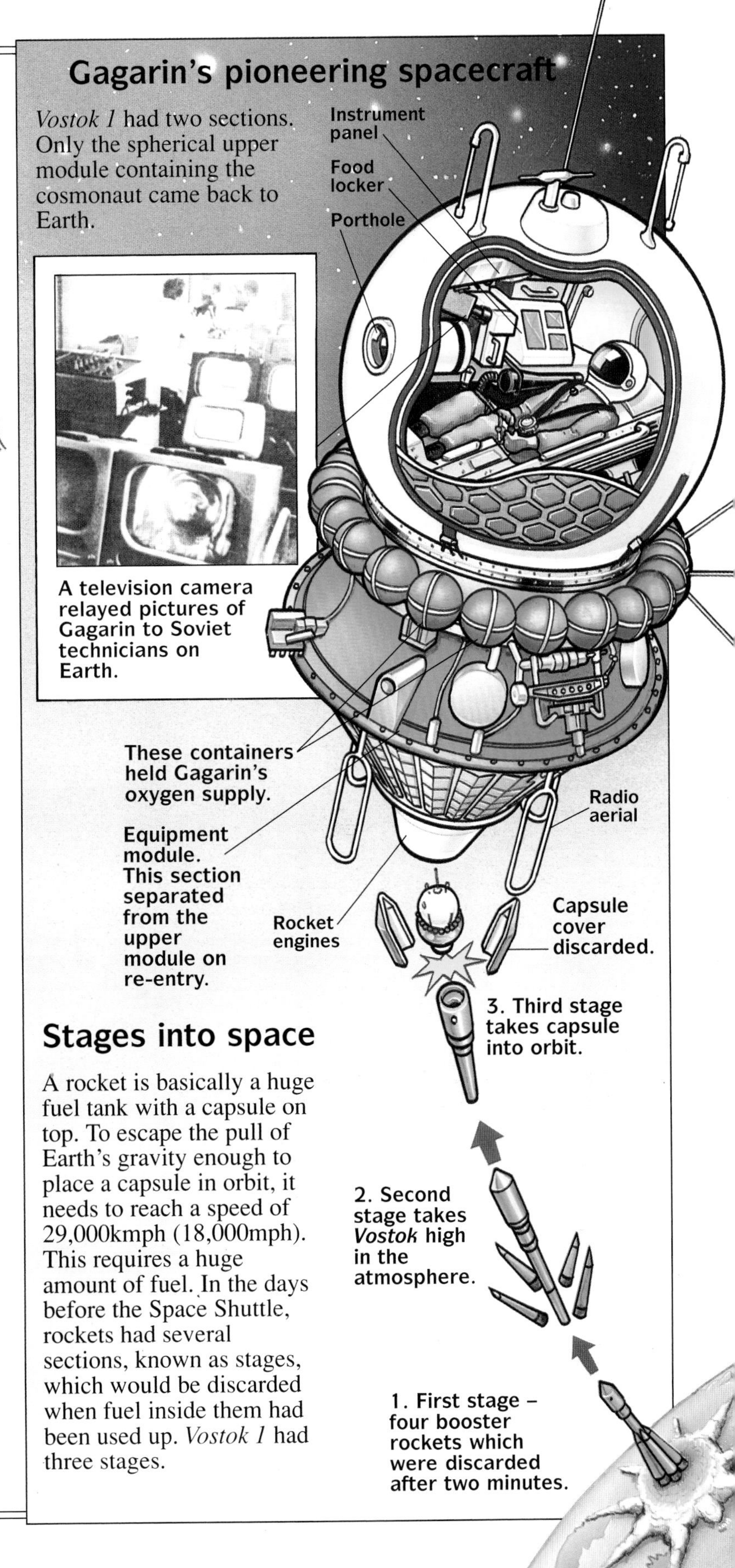

A television camera relayed pictures of Gagarin to Soviet technicians on Earth.

Stages into space

A rocket is basically a huge fuel tank with a capsule on top. To escape the pull of Earth's gravity enough to place a capsule in orbit, it needs to reach a speed of 29,000kmph (18,000mph). This requires a huge amount of fuel. In the days before the Space Shuttle, rockets had several sections, known as stages, which would be discarded when fuel inside them had been used up. *Vostok 1* had three stages.

The crushing sensation began to lessen as *Vostok 1* gradually escaped the clutches of gravity, and entered into orbit around the Earth. Gagarin was now flying at 8km (5 miles) a second.

Rising in his chair as far as his harness would allow he immediately became aware of the sensation of weightlessness. At first he found it unpleasant, but adapted very quickly. It was not nearly as disorienting as scientists had feared. He unbuckled his belt, and hung in the air, between floor and ceiling. It felt as though his arms and legs did not belong to him, and his map case, pencil and note pad floated by. The whole sensation was very dreamlike. Strangest of all was the way in which liquids behaved. Water leaking from a drink container took on a spherical shape and floated in midair until it reached a solid surface where it settled like dew on a flower.

Cat out of bag

Once he was safely in space, the Soviet authorities decided to release the news to an unsuspecting world. Radio Moscow interrupted its usual schedule with a burst of patriotic music, and a solemn voice which announced: "The world's first spaceship with a man on board has been launched in the Soviet Union on a round-the-world orbit." Throughout the country, factory, farm and office workers listened intently, scarcely believing that their nation had performed such a scientific miracle.

Gagarin kept detailed notes of what it was like to be weightless. He was fascinated by the way water floated into spherical droplets.

High altitude report

Up in orbit, there was very little actual flying to be done. Flight corrections were made automatically. The discarding of stages, the flight path and speed of the capsule, even the conditions inside the cabin, were all controlled from the ground, or by computer. This left Gagarin free to concentrate on what he saw and felt. He quickly realized that weightlessness was not going to affect the way he worked, so he began to jot down observations and report what he could see.

The orbit of *Vostok 1* took it between 181km (112 miles) and 327km (203 miles) above the surface of the Earth. From here coastlines, mountain ranges and forests could easily be seen, as well as the curve of the Earth. Along this curve the pale blue atmosphere gradually darkened in a series of incredibly rich hues – from turquoise to blue, violet and finally black. Above this beautiful sight hung the dark eternity of space. For Gagarin, who was brought up on a farm, space looked like "a huge black field sown with star-like grain."

Day to night

The sun looked very different. Without the Earth's atmosphere to soften its rays it seemed a hundred times brighter. It reminded Gagarin of molten metal, and when it shone directly into his capsule he had to shield his portholes with protective filters.

Suddenly *Vostok 1* plunged into pitch dark as the capsule flew out of the rays of the sun and behind the shaded side of the Earth. Below, Gagarin could see only blackness, but concluded he must be flying over an ocean.

Although the cosmonaut was neither hungry not thirsty he

ate a small meal – carefully sucking pulped food from a tube-like container, and drinking a little water. He had to be careful transferring both food and liquid from container to mouth, in case it floated off and attached itself to his instrument panels.

Soon *Vostok 1* emerged again into the light, the horizon blazing from bright orange through all the colours of the rainbow. Having reported carefully the new sensations and sights he was seeing, Gagarin's mind began to wander. Alone in his capsule, more remote and out of reach than any human ever before, he thought of the bustling streets of Moscow, where he had visited his wife and two daughters a couple of days before the flight.

Back to Earth

In less than 90 minutes *Vostok 1* had orbited the entire Earth, and now it was time to return. This was the most dangerous part of the flight. If something had gone wrong at takeoff, there was a small chance of ejecting to safety. If anything went wrong now, the first man in space could be marooned forever, or burned to a cinder. Until this time, Gagarin had had every faith in his spacecraft, but now he began to wonder if it would work properly. Was there some unforeseen danger lurking on the return journey?

On board equipment oriented the capsule in the correct flight path, using the Sun as a guide, and *Vostok 1* began its giddy descent. As it plunged inexorably down into the upper layers of the atmosphere the outer skin of the craft began to glow red hot. Fiery crimson flames flashed past his small portholes, as Gagarin was once again pinned to his seat.

Coming back was much more unpleasant than going out, and when his ship began to tumble around he became intensely worried.

Near disaster

Things had in fact gone seriously wrong. Before re-entry his small capsule was supposed to separate from a connected equipment module (see diagram on page 57). Unknown to Gagarin this had not happened correctly, and both craft were still attached by electrical wiring. Fortunately the heat of re-entry burned away the wire cables, the two craft separated, and disaster was averted.

The rotation finally stopped, the descent parachutes opened to slow down the speeding capsule, and Gagarin realized that the worst was over. He had risked his life for the glory of his country and he was going to live to tell the tale. Overcome with joy he began to sing at the top of his voice.

There remained one final, dangerous step. 6,000m (20,000ft) from the ground his couch ejected from the capsule, and he floated back to Earth by parachute. Soviet rocket engineers thought that landing inside the capsule would be too jarring, and parachuting down separately was safer.

At 10:55, less than two hours after he had taken off, Gagarin landed in a field near the village of Smelovka, watched by two startled farm workers. They walked toward him, eager to help, but slowed uncertainly as they approached. His unfamiliar bright orange spacesuit and large white helmet clearly frightened them.

One, a woman named Anna Takhtarova, asked "Are you from outer space?" Taking off his helmet Gagarin reassured her that he was a fellow human, but, yes, he had come from outer space. Then other farm workers arrived. Unlike Takharova, they had been listening to their radio. "It's Yuri Gagarin! It's Yuri Gagarin!" one shouted, completely astonished to be meeting the remarkable man he had heard about minutes before.

Then, elated astronaut and the excited farm workers embraced and kissed like long-lost relatives. This was indeed an extraordinary moment. For the first time in history a man had left the planet and returned safely to Earth.

Above. Gagarin is acclaimed by Soviet leader Nikita Khrushchev. Left. Medal of Pilot-Cosmonaut of the Soviet Union.

Heroes on film

Around half the stories in this book have featured in films which you can still see from time to time on television, or rent from a video store. Here are some of the best.

Reliving her ordeal

Odette Sansom's work with the French Resistance, and her subsequent capture and imprisonment, was portrayed in the 1950 film *Odette*. British actress Anna Neagle played the French secret agent.

The film was partially shot at Fresnes Prison, Paris, where Odette herself had been held prisoner. She worked as an advisor on the project, but seeing the film's actors relive her worst moments was a painful experience.

Anna Neagle in *Odette*. Here, feigning kindness, a Gestapo officer offers a cigarette prior to a torture session.

From psycho to sympathy

Geronimo has fascinated film makers for most of the century and scores of films featuring him have been made. The first picture about him, *Geronimo's Last Raid* was shot in 1912, only three years after his death.

As the years passed his depiction on screen changed from that of a bloodthirsty savage to a much-wronged hero. In 1939 the poster for *Geronimo!* proclaimed "Ten thousand Red Raiders roar into battle!" *Geronimo*, made in 1993, on the other hand, takes a much more sympathetic look at the Apache people and their tragic demise.

Wes Studi plays the Apache warrior in *Geronimo*.

The Right Rocket

Chuck Yeager's assault on the sound barrier was captured spectacularly in the 1983 American film *The Right Stuff*. Based on Tom Wolfe's best-selling book of the same title, the film also depicts America's first efforts to place a man in space. Yeager worked as a technical advisor on the film, and also made a brief appearance as a bartender at an inn near Muroc airbase.

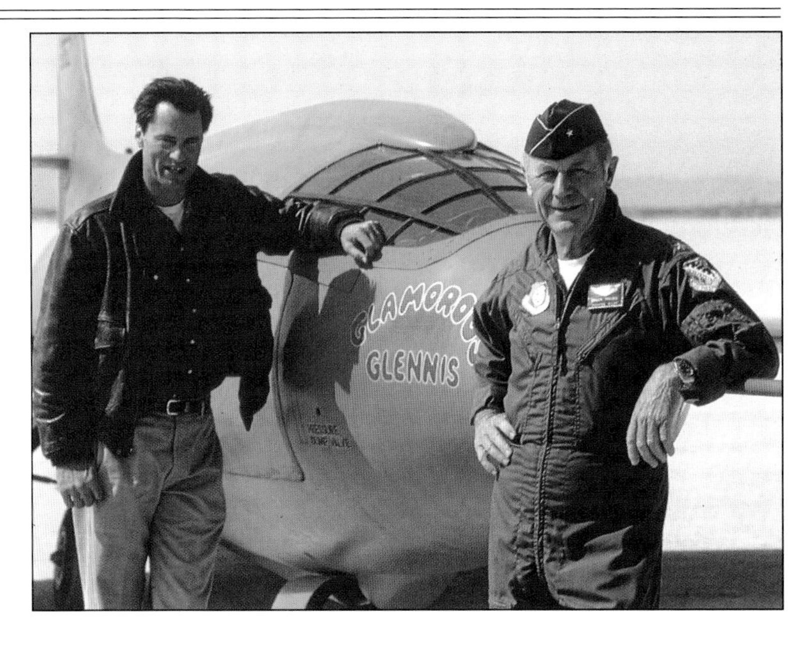

Chuck Yeager with actor Sam Shepard, who plays him in the film. Behind them is a plywood mock-up of Yeager's X-1 rocket.

Owens' Berlin victory

Jesse Owens' Olympic triumph was captured on film by eminent German director Leni Riefenstahl in *Olympische Spiele 1936*.

This sinister but beautiful film is seen by many as a hymn to Germany's racist Nazi regime, but Riefenstahl made no attempt to play down African-American Owens' victories over Germany's athletes.

In this still from Leni Riefenstahl's *Olympische Spiele 1936* the Berlin Olympic Stadium is encircled by columns of searchlights. Spectacular visual displays such as this were also used to great effect during Nazi Party rallies.

Maynard written out

In the 1952 American film *Blackbeard the Pirate* Robert Newton played the infamous plunderer, charging around waving pistols and rolling his eyes with immense enthusiasm. The plot takes great liberties with the known facts. Instead of Lieutenant Maynard, reformed villain Sir Henry Morgan is hired to rid the high seas of the evil pirate. Morgan still has something of a wicked streak in him and Blackbeard comes to a suitably gruesome end. Buried up to his neck on a sandy beach he is slowly drowned by the incoming tide.

Robert Newton in *Blackbeard the Pirate*. Newton was employed to roll his eyes in much the same way in another pirate film, *Long John Silver*.

After the event

Chernobyl

(Terror stalks Chernobyl, p.14)

To prevent further radiation escaping, a huge concrete casing was constructed around the ruptured number four reactor. However, local scientists are concerned that an earthquake could cause this to collapse. For 30km (20 miles) around Chernobyl, farmland lies in ruins, and deserted towns slowly crumble and decay. 135,000 people had to evacuate the area, never to return. Today, illnesses caused by exposure to radiation from the explosion continue to claim lives.

Pauline Cutting

(Rubble and strife in battlefield Beirut, p.50)

In 1987 Cutting was awarded the OBE (Order of the British Empire) by the British government in recognition of her work in Bourj al Barajneh. She is a member of the board of Medical Aid for Palestinians, and returned to Beirut in October 1995, while reviewing the charity's projects in Lebanon.

She now works in a hospital in Amsterdam, and is married to **Ben Alofs**. They have two children. **Susie Wighton** was awarded an MBE (Member of the British Empire) in 1987. She still works as an emergency relief worker and spent much of 1995 in Rwanda.

Yuri Gagarin

(Cosmonaut number one, p.56)

Gagarin's 1961 spaceflight made him an instant celebrity, and he spent the next five years touring the world, even visiting the Soviet Union's arch rival the United States. He was an excellent ambassador for his country, and his amiable modesty made him hugely popular with the thousands who turned out to see him.

In 1968 he began to train for another spaceflight, but was killed when a jet he was flying hit the ground as it swerved to avoid another aircraft which had flown too close. A massive funeral ceremony was held in Moscow, and Gagarin's remains were buried in the Kremlin wall.

Bob Geldof

(Boomtown Bob's global jukebox, p.4)

Live Aid raised £40 million ($70 million) for the Ethiopian famine and remains the most successful charity concert ever staged. Half the money was spent on food, and half went to long-term projects such as road building, irrigation, farming, and sanitation schemes.

Geldof lives in London. He still records and performs from time to time, and also runs the *Planet 24* television company. He returned to Ethiopia in 1995, to make a documentary with BBC television, marking the tenth anniversary of Live Aid. Recalling the impact of the concerts on those who donated money, he told British magazine *Radio Times*, "There was an absolute awareness that you were not powerless in the face of massive events. The individual could make a change."

Ethiopia is still a very poor country, although the civil war, a major cause of the famine, ended in 1991.

Geronimo

(Geronimo's final stand, p.22)

Geronimo spent his last years coming to terms with the society he had fought so hard to resist. He tried farming and Christianity, but was expelled from his church because he refused to give up gambling.

If anyone was going to exploit his notoriety, Geronimo was determined it was going to be him. He sold his photograph to those who flocked to shows and circuses to see him, for a then exorbitant two dollars.

The US Army, in a curious compliment to their old enemy, adopted his name as a warcry. During World War Two paratroops yelled "Geronimo" as they plunged from their aircraft and into battle.

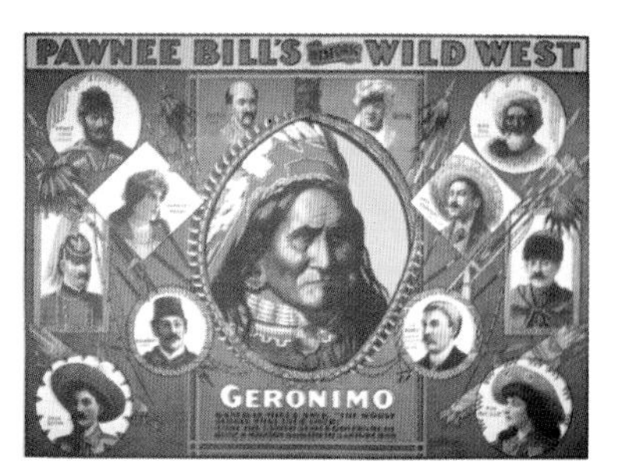

Geronimo is the main attraction in this 1904 poster advertising "Pawnee Bill's Wild West Show".

Chico Mendes

(Brazil's rainforest hero, p.27)

Following the 1989 election Mendes' friend **José Lutzenberger** became Brazilian Minister for the Environment. Further road building into the Amazon was cancelled, and strict laws limiting burning of the forest were enforced. Vast areas of forest were set aside for conservation, including a 800,000 hectare (two million acre) region named in memory of Mendes.

Jesse Owens

(Owens' Olympic triumph, p.18)

When the Games ended, the athletes' Olympic village was turned into an army training camp, and anti-Jewish propaganda reappeared in the German media. Hitler fantasized that following the Nazi conquest of Europe the Games would be held in Germany forever, and black athletes would be forbidden to compete.

Jesse Owens' long jump record remained unbeaten until 1960, but his fame did not bring him happiness. Deluged with show business and business offers, Owens displayed his athletic ability at sideshows and exhibitions, where he would run against racehorses, or play with the novelty basketball team *The Harlem Globetrotters*. The money he made was invested in businesses that collapsed.

After the Second World War his life improved. He worked for children's charities and went around the world as a goodwill ambassador for the United States. He died in 1980.

Owens' friend and Olympic rival **Lutz Long** was killed in 1943, fighting with the German army in Sicily.

Odette Sansom

(Odette's ordeal, p.32)

Following her release Odette returned to England. She had several operations on her injured feet before she was able to walk without discomfort. In 1946 she became the first woman to be given the George Cross, Britain's highest civilian award for bravery.

In 1948 she married **Peter Churchill**, the man she had suffered so much to protect. But after eight years they parted, and Odette married Geoffrey Hallowes, another former secret agent. In later life she co-founded the British "Woman of the Year" award, worked for charities, and spent many hours writing to thousands of people with problems, who had contacted her for advice or inspiration. She died in 1995, aged 82.

Mary Seacole

(Mother Seacole's Balaclava boys, p.38)

Seacole returned to England ruined by the collapse of her trading business, and set about writing her biography to make some money. "*Wonderful adventures of Mrs. Seacole in Many Lands*" was published in 1857, and its success brought some financial security. She spent the rest of her days living in Jamaica and England and became friends with members of the British royal family, who called on her medical skills to treat their ailments. She died in 1881 aged 77.

Stauffenberg

(Stauffenberg's Secret Germany, p.42)

Had Stauffenberg and his conspirators succeeded with *Operation Valkyrie* the war in Europe might have ended much earlier. As it was, it continued for almost another year.

Hitler described the conspiracy as "a crime unparalleled in German history" and reacted accordingly. Although Stauffenberg, **Olbricht, Haeften**, and **von Quirnheim** were dead and buried, Hitler demanded that their bodies be burned and the ashes scattered to the wind.

Following brutal interrogation the main surviving conspirators were hauled before the Nazi courts. They refused to be intimidated and knew the regime they loathed was teetering on the brink of defeat. General **Erich Fellgiebel**, who had stood with Stauffenberg as the bomb exploded at Rastenburg, was told by the Court President that he was to be hanged. "Hurry with the hanging Mr. President," he replied, "otherwise you will hang earlier than we."

Gestapo and SS officers investigated the plot until the last days of the war. Seven thousand arrests were made and between two and three thousand people were executed.

Stauffenberg's personal magnetism continued to exert an extraordinary influence, even from beyond the grave. SS investigator Georg Kiesel was so in awe of him he reported to Hitler that his would-be assassin was "a spirit of fire, fascinating and inspiring all who came in touch with him."

Chuck Yeager

(Punching a hole in the sky, p.10)

News of Yeager's top secret X-1 flight was released to the world in December 1947. Showered with awards and accolades, he continued working as a test pilot, pioneering supersonic flight.

In the 1960s he returned to active service, flying bombing missions over Vietnam. After retirement Yeager spent his time hunting, flying (anything from gliders to high speed jets), and making regular appearances as an after-dinner speaker. "I'm not the rocking-chair type," he remarked in his 1986 autobiography *Yeager*.

Further reading

If you would like to know more about some of these stories, the following books contain useful information.

Ablaze – the story of Chernobyl by Piers Paul Reid (Secker 1993)
Animal Heroes by Yvonne Roberts (Pelham, 1990)
Bury My Heart At Wounded Knee (An Indian History of the American West) by Dee Brown (Vintage, 1991)
Children of the Siege by Pauline Cutting (Heinemann, 1988)
Is That It? by Bob Geldof (Sidgwick & Jackson, 1986)
The July Plot by Nigel Richardson (Dryad Press Ltd, 1986)
Odette by Jerrard Tickell (New Portaway, 1949)
Odette Churchill by Catherine Sanders (Hamish Hamilton, 1989)
Jesse Owens by Tony Gentry (Melrose Square Publishing Company, 1990)
The Pirates by Douglas Botting (Time-Life Books, 1978)
The Space Race by Jon Trux (New English Library, 1985)
Wonderful Adventures of Mrs Seacole in many lands by Mary Seacole (Oxford University Press, 1988)
Yeager – An Autobiography by Chuck Yeager and Leo Janos (Century, 1989)

Acknowledgements and photo credits

The Publishers would like to thank the following for their help and advice:

Dr. David Killingray, Reader in History, Goldsmiths College, University of London; Medical Aid for Palestinians and Pauline Cutting; Doug Millard, Associate Curator for Space Technology, Science Museum, London; Mark Seaman, Imperial War Museum, London.

The Publishers would like to thank the following for permission to reproduce these photographs in this book: Band Aid Trust, London (5 bottom); David Brenchley/Cornish Photo News (cover, bottom right, 37 inset); Coldstream Guards (by permission of the Regimental Lieutenant Colonel) (30 bottom); Edwards Airforce Base, California – History Office Flight Test Center (3 top left, 11, 12, 13); Gedenkstätte Deutscher Widerstand, Berlin (42 bottom right, 44, 46); Hulton Deutsch, London (19, 32, 38 bottom, 45 top right, 50, 56 top, 59); Imperial War Museum, London (40 bottom); David King Collection, London, (55 bottom); The Kobal Collection, London (60 top, Herbert Wilcox, 60 bottom, Columbia, 61 top, Warner/Ladd (Irwin Winkler, Robert Chartoff) 61 bottom left, Leni Riefenstahl, 61 bottom right, RKO (Edmund Grainger); London Express News & Features/Evening Standard/Maurice Conroy (8 middle); London Features International – Frank Griffin (9 bottom) Steve Rapport (back cover); Mansell Collection, London (39); Mirror Syndication International, London (4 top); National Archives Still Picture Branch, Maryland (24-25, 26); Peter Newark Historical Pictures, Bath (22, 49 middle, 62); Novosti, London (14 middle, 55 top, 56 bottom); Novosti Photo Library/V. Samokhotsky (15); Ronnie O'Brien, (21); Ohio State University Photo Archives (18, 20 top); Popperfoto, Northampton (42 bottom middle); Punch Magazine, London (40 middle); The Quaker Oats Company, Chicago (30 top); Range/Bettmann/UPI, London (10, 20 bottom); Rex Features Ltd, London, (6 bottom, 7, 9 top, 9 middle, 28, 29, 53, 54 bottom); Rex Features/Sipa Press (17, 28, 54 top); Frank Spooner Pictures, London (16); Frank Spooner/Gamma (4 bottom); Frank Spooner/Gamma/Sigla (27); Frank Spooner/Gamma/Françoise Demulder (52); ©T. Stone – all proceeds from the use of these photographs go to the Multiple Sclerosis Society (cover top, 37); Topham Picture Source (36); Wiener Library, London (34-35 bottom, 42 bottom left, 42 top);

Picture research: Charlotte Deane

The illustrations of Band Aid and Live Aid symbols which appear in this book are used by permission of the Band Aid Trust, London.

Index

First published in 1996 by Usborne Publishing Ltd, Usborne House, 83-85 Saffron Hill, London EC1N 8RT.
First published in America August 1996

Printed in Spain UE